Vicki Blum

The Land Without Unicorns

Cover by Pat Stephens

Illustrated by David Bordeleau

Scholastic Canada Ltd.

Toronto New York London Auckland Sydney
Mexico City New Delhi Hong Kong

Scholastic Canada Ltd.
175 Hillmount Road, Markham, Ontario, Canada L6C 1Z7

Scholastic Inc.
555 Broadway, New York, NY 10012, USA

Scholastic Australia Pty Limited
PO Box 579, Gosford, NSW 2250, Australia

Scholastic New Zealand Limited
Private Bag 94407, Greenmount, Auckland, New Zealand

Scholastic Ltd.
Villiers House, Clarendon Avenue, Leamington Spa,
Warwickshire CV32 5PR, UK

Map by Paul Heersink/Paperglyphs

Edited by Laura Peetoom

National Library of Canada Cataloguing in Publication Data

Blum, Vicki, 1955–
The land without unicorns

ISBN 0-439-98863-2

I. Bordeleau, David. II. Title.

PS8553.L86L36 2001   jC813'.54   C2001-930286-X
PZ7.B48La 2001

5 4 3 2 1   Printed and bound in Canada   1 2 3 4 5/0

To my brother Scott, who encouraged me to write

"Will the unicorn be willing to serve thee . . . ?"
Job 39:9

The Borderlands
of North
& South Bundelag

Ogre
Forest

North Bundelag

The Black Badlands

Fairy
Village

River of Songs

Entrance
from Earth

Little River

Tak

Lake Tak

East-West Road

Mulek

South Bundelag

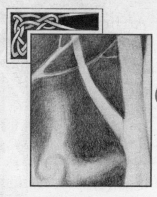

Chapter 1

Arica had only been in Bundelag a few moments when she realized Connor had followed her through the crack between the worlds.

Her cousin was not supposed to be here. But then, when was Connor ever where he was supposed to be? Or *not* where he was *not* supposed to be? Right now, the place he was clearly not supposed to be was here in North Bundelag, where humans had not been allowed to come for over four hundred years.

Grandmother had asked Arica to take care of her house while she was away. Unfortunately, Connor was in from the ranch for a visit and when she mentioned she had to water the plants and feed the lizards, he begged to come along. At first she did very well at keeping him out of the kitchen and away from the crack. But when she felt something calling to her from the cellar she had to just push him out the door.

Now here he was behind her, already through the tunnel and into the woods. He stood in her tracks, while the doorway from Earth blinked out behind them, and stared back with goggle eyes at the place where it had been.

She wondered briefly if she could get away with dragging him rapidly back the way they had come and telling him that it had all been a bad dream. But the idea was quashed the next moment when Wish bounded gleefully out from behind a tree and into the small clearing where they stood. The unicorn stopped, stared at the boy, flicked her tail and snorted. Connor stared back, his mouth gaping. Wish did a little dance through the foliage, tossed her head at a passing bumblebee and landed on four feet at Arica's side.

A boy followed you through the crack, she said, and nipped playfully at Arica's sleeve.

"You're kidding," Arica teased, stroking a nose as soft as rose petals.

No, True Arica, I am not kidding, Wish replied seriously. *The boy is standing right behind you.* Then she spotted a little orange butterfly and bounced away.

"I know, Wish!" Arica called out after her. "I was being sarcastic. Do you know what that means? Oh, never mind. I'm in deep trouble, you know. I've been careless, and Connor is here, and the Fairy Queen will never forgive me!"

Connor, who had been standing stone-still and speechless since his arrival in Bundelag, finally regained his voice — or at least some of it. The highest part, anyway.

"Why are you talking to the filly like that?" he shrilled at her. "Everyone knows animals can't talk back! And why does she have a horn? Is this some kind of joke? You should know better than try to fool me! I've been around horses all of my life!"

Then he took off after Wish — for a better look at the horn, Arica presumed. It was beyond her how Connor figured she would go to all the work of sticking a horn on a horse, just to fool him. He neared the animal, his skinny arms flying, as usual showing twice as much gusto as was needed.

When Wish saw Connor flouncing and flapping toward her, she snorted in alarm. Her next action was purely instinctive. A spurt of blue light — barely a flicker, really — burst from the tip of her horn and bounced off the boy's chest. The jolt likely surprised him more than it hurt. He cried out and leaped backward, tripped over a fallen tree branch, tumbled head-over-heels, and landed bottom-down in a nearby patch of prickle bush.

Arica was extremely proud of herself for not laughing right out loud. As it was, the effort to choke down her mirth brought tears to her eyes and robbed her of her breath. She turned her head the other way and pretended to watch the antics of Wish's orange butterfly. A few moments went by before she could trust herself to look up or to speak. By that time Connor had managed to dig himself out of the bush and was standing in front of her, glaring angrily through his bottle-bottom glasses.

"Why didn't you tell me about this place?" he demanded. His face was getting redder with every word, and his voice louder. "You have a lot of explaining to do! I thought we were friends. I thought I was your favourite cousin. You know — no secrets, and all of that stuff!"

"Well, I — "

"I will never trust you again!" he howled, and stomped away.

Arica watched him go, feeling a little ashamed. It was true that she was his best friend. In fact, she had come to realize lately that it was possible she was his only friend.

Connor didn't seem to fit in well with other children. He was small and thin, like a person made of sticks and string, and when he got excited, which was about half of the time, he squeaked like a baby

. . . landed bottom-down in a nearby patch of prickle bush.

bird. He couldn't ski down a hill and he couldn't skate. He was too short for basketball and too slight for football. In water, he sank like a stone. Even at soccer, he was nearly hopeless. The two months she spent last spring playing the game with him had revealed to her just how many ways one boy could trip, tumble or slide down a soccer field without ever getting the ball anywhere near the net.

But he could ride, and when he climbed on a fast horse, you might as well wave goodbye. She had always been proud of him for that. He was, after all, the only cousin she had living nearby.

"Wait!" she called. "Don't leave!"

The only thing worse than bringing Connor to Bundelag would be losing Connor in Bundelag. How would she ever explain something like that to her aunt and uncle? For that matter, would they even believe her? Once let loose, there was no telling how much damage Connor could do to this place, or it to him.

Where was Connor now? He had disappeared altogether. Arica scrambled toward the spot where she had last seen him. "Wait!" she cried again.

The next moment he burst back out of the bushes right in front of her, white-faced and wild-eyed, his hands flapping at his sides like paddles. She dived out of the way just in time to avoid hitting him head-on. He tore on past like he didn't even noticed she was there.

She whirled around and shouted his name. After a few more metres he skidded to a halt, seeming to realize for the first time that he had no idea where to go.

He stood poised, trembling and looking very confused, like he was caught between the desire to flee and the realization that he was nearly lost already. He compromised by dashing to the nearest tree trunk and ducking behind it.

Now Arica heard hooves beating on earth and the crackle of tortured underbrush. She whirled back again just in time to see two enormous dapple-grey stallions prance out into the clearing. They snorted when they saw her and flung back their fine, proud heads. Silken manes lapped like waves against their arching necks.

On top of the first stallion sat Nue the elf, someone she knew well. The second stallion carried on its back none other than her own dear grandmother, the Fairy Queen of North Bundelag. Arica tried to imagine what this colourful apparition must have looked like to Connor. First there were the two enormous stallions, as big as the draft horses of home, without saddle or bridle, guided only by the touch of their riders' knees. Then there was Nue, a frightening sight even when he was on the ground, with his huge head, big pointed ears and saucer-wide eyes. But mounted and suddenly bursting out from the forest right on top of you? He would rattle the teeth of anyone, brave or not. And poor Connor had never seen any elf until this moment, much less one so lacking in the delicate beauty most elves possessed.

Then there was Grandmother.

For some reason the Fairy Queen had arrived in full fairy costume. A long purple robe flowed from her shoulders and down over her ankles. A silver wand rested in her right hand. A sword dangled at her side. But this was the first time Arica had ever seen her wearing a crown.

It was a tiny golden thing that glittered with jewels of every colour imaginable. It was nestled in Grandmother's hair like a tiny halo of light that sent sparkles of fire dancing through the treetops overhead.

To Connor, Arica's grandmother was just Mrs. Warman, someone he met on birthdays or at other family gatherings. Connor and Arica were related because their mothers were sisters, so this grandmother — her father's mother — had no blood tie with him. But she had always treated him with friendliness and respect — at home, at least. Arica wasn't sure how long that friendliness would last when the Fairy Queen discovered Connor here in North Bundelag. She wondered how long she could count on Connor staying hidden behind his maple tree.

Nue peered down at her from his perch on the horse.

"Dear Arica!" he exclaimed, wagging one pudgy, dirt-stained hand in greeting. "It's so good to see you, companion of my last great adventure!" His gaze settled on Wish. "And you, too, little unicorn, friend to the courageous Arica! It seems like only yesterday we defeated the mighty one-eyed ogres, outran the great dark wolf of the forest, traversed the terrible Badlands to confront the wicked fairy Raden and his friend, the shadow unicorn . . ."

"It's good to see you, too," Arica interrupted. She did not usually break into the middle of someone's sentence, but once Nue got going, there was no telling when he would finally wind down. With him, everything seemed to have grown to excess, including his way of remembering an event: grander and greater with every retelling. They hadn't exactly defeated the ogres, though they had eventually befriended them, and they certainly hadn't outrun the wolf. She feared that if he told this tale too many more times, he might abandon the facts altogether.

Then Arica looked past Nue again to the woman seated so majestically upon the other horse.

"Hello, Grandmother," she said, trying not to think about Connor. It was impossible to keep a secret from Grandmother for more than ten seconds. Every once in a while it seemed the old woman could read her thoughts, just like the unicorns did. Fortunately, as Fairy Queen of North Bundelag, Grandmother frequently had too much on her mind to really focus on Arica's. Arica saw that this was one of those times. Worry lines ran deep across her brow, and her attention seemed fixed on some distant place rather than on what was going on around her.

"Dear child," she said, "I asked Wish to call you back to Bundelag to do a very important task. The sooner you go, the better. I can trust this only to a fairy, and Doron, the Keeper of the village, is too old and frail."

The way she said it made Arica's heart flip up to her throat. There must be great danger involved. It was obvious the Fairy Queen hadn't made this decision lightly.

"What is it?" she managed to force out, her voice barely above a whisper, all thoughts of Connor having flown from her mind.

Grandmother slid from the stallion's back in one quick, graceful movement, as befitted the fairy queen she was. Nue, on the other hand, caught his jacket button in the stallion's mane, dangled against its neck yelping and struggling while the horse pranced wildly, tore free, then belly-flopped into the prickle bush.

Grandmother was too preoccupied to even glance

in Nue's direction. "A long time ago," she explained, "a very special book was made. It was called the *Book of Fairies*. It was written by the greatest and wisest of our people, and much love and magic went into its creation. It contained our learning and our laws. But even more important, a spell was woven into the book so that every time one with fairy blood was born, his or her name appeared inside."

"A fairy genealogy?" Arica asked.

Grandmother shook her head. "No, there were other books for listing family trees and recording history. This book only kept a record of living fairies. Once a fairy died, his or her name faded from the page. As you have probably guessed, this book was unique. Obeying the laws written there brought us great happiness and increased our abilities to use magic for good. It contained most of our recipes and spells, many of which are now forgotten."

An uneasy feeling was beginning to creep through Arica's bones. "Was the book destroyed?"

Grandmother shook her head. "No, something even more terrible happened. It was lost during the Great War. The good news is the book was recently found. The bad news is this: it is in South Bundelag, in the hands of a wealthy human merchant who will not be eager to give it up.

"I need someone to travel to South Bundelag and bring it back. If the book's magic is still at work —

and I have no reason to think it is not — then it should give us the names of the fairies lost on Earth. I believe this will help us to find them.

"Will you do this for me, and for your own people, dear Granddaughter?"

Just as she opened her mouth to say "of course," a shrill cry of "I will!" came from behind the tree.

Chapter 2

The quick intake of Grandmother's breath hissed through the still morning. Nue turned toward the sound with obvious interest, as though not wanting to miss what might happen next. Wish lifted her nose from the blossoms, sensing the sudden tension in the air, and peered at them all with perked ears.

"I didn't mean — " Arica started to say, but Grandmother interrupted her before she had the chance to explain.

"Who is behind the tree?" the old lady demanded, each word dropping like a stone. "And how did he get here?"

Arica had to give Connor credit — he had used

the minutes he was hidden to gather his courage. She watched with bated breath as her cousin stepped out into full view with his chin up. He faced Grandmother bravely, his thin face pale but determined. A smear of dirt blackened one cheek and the tip of his nose, and bits of broken leaves fluttered like plume moths in his hair. Light from Grandmother's crown sparkled off the lenses of his glasses, which hung lopsided from his nose.

"I'm happy to meet you again, Mrs. Warman," he said, his voice only a little high and shaky. "Please don't be angry with Arica. It's not her fault that I'm here in this secret place — really, it isn't. I went to your house with her to water your plants. She tried to get rid of me, but . . . "

Grandmother received this explanation with silence — the kind that always made Arica want to babble. It had the same effect on Connor.

"I love your house. It's so warm and . . . and magical-feeling. So when she pushed me out I came back in and hid. Then I fell through the floor, and when I saw Arica disappear into the tunnel, I went after her."

"I see," said Grandmother coolly, her eyebrows lifting just a millimetre. This, actually, was a good sign. With Grandmother, the lower the eyebrows, the greater the displeasure. Once they started rising, there was hope. And Connor was being honest and sincere, which was exactly the right thing to do.

"I can be a lot of help if you just give me a chance," he continued eagerly. "I can ride." He nodded at the stallions. "And I'm very good at finding things. Just last week I found a lost calf of my father's that had been missing for a whole day."

"Is that so?" said Grandmother, her eyebrows rising at least another centimetre.

"Good Queen," spoke up Nue. "Perhaps you should take up the boy on his offer. It is a dangerous task that you have assigned to Arica, and although there are none to equal your noble granddaughter in agility and courage, it would be safer for her to have another person along. Not, perhaps, as safe as if I were there, but this boy seems willing and able, and I sense goodness in him."

"You don't need to tell me about Connor," the Fairy Queen said irritably. "I've known him all of his short life, and there's nothing wrong with him except that he shouldn't be here in Bundelag!"

There was a brief pause. It was a chance, finally, for Arica to explain herself. "I didn't mean for this to happen," she said quickly, before someone could start talking again. "I thought he had gone home, but then there he was, right behind me. That's no excuse, of course. I wasn't careful enough, and I'm sorry."

Grandmother's face softened as she looked at

Arica. "Perhaps I am being a bit harsh," she admitted. "But these are difficult times for Bundelag. There is so much danger, and so much to worry about. Small battles are still breaking out all along the border, and the elves are not yet unified."

Her gaze fell upon Connor once again. The boy pushed his glasses back up his nose and looked back at her bravely.

"I can help," he insisted. "I know I can."

Grandmother nodded thoughtfully, one fingertip resting lightly on her chin. "I believe you would do your best, Connor. And you're right, Nue. It would be safer for Arica with her cousin along." She reached out and took Arica's hand in hers. "It seems we never have enough time together, dear Granddaughter." She smiled sadly. "I have to go now. The ogres have requested that I meet with them. They are officially joining us in our war against the South. But with ogres, there will be a lot of pomp and ceremony to get through before the agreement is finally reached." She sighed. "Politics are necessary, but often tiresome."

Then Grandmother pulled the silver sword from its sheath.

"Take your father's sword and keep it with you at all times. South Bundelag is not a friendly place."

Arica took the sword and hooked it onto her belt. It had served her well once before, and although its

Then Grandmother pulled the sliver sword from its sheath.

magic was not all-powerful, it did give some degree of protection. Grandmother hugged her, brushed a stray lock of hair from Arica's eyes, and turned away. One of the great, grey stallions dropped to its knees. She mounted and it rose, its fine, intelligent head thrown back, its long legs prancing, eager to be gone.

"Nue has supplies, and will fill you in on all the details of your journey," Grandmother said as her horse moved away. "I have patrols stationed along the border, but I have sent word instructing them to let you through. Nue will explain about the bridge when you get there. Connor, you may remain in Bundelag, but only until you and Arica return to me with the *Book of Fairies*." She paused and added, half to herself, "I hope I don't live to regret this."

Then she and both of the stallions disappeared into the forest with a rattle of hooves and a crackle of underbrush that slowly died away to silence. Connor stared after them.

A moment later Nue waddled up to the boy and bowed. "Pleased to meet you, young lad," he said gushingly. "Any friend of Arica's is a friend of mine!"

Connor dragged his dumbfounded gaze back to the little man standing in front of him. "Who are you?" he asked, staring at Nue's ears. "What are you? I've never seen anyone like you before."

"Well, then — it's time we explained some things," the elf said.

So they sat in the grass and munched on dry berries and nuts (Nue's version of trail mix) while Arica made the formal introductions and told Connor all about this land called Bundelag. She told him how the elves in the North were fighting for their freedom against the humans in the South. She described how the ogres had joined in, and how she and Grandmother needed to find the lost fairies or they would never be able to win the war. She explained to him how her own father was actually a fairy lost on Earth without any memory of his magic. Lastly, she told him about the unicorns. She called Wish over, and Connor touched her nose and smoothed her silk-soft mane.

After that, Nue mentioned that they should get going — that they had a long way to travel and not much time. He commended Arica for her foresight in bringing her knapsack (she always brought a packed one to Grandmother's, just in case) and then packed it even fuller with some of the supplies he had brought. The heaviest ones, she noticed.

"This place is the best," Connor said later as they trudged through the forest after Nue. "I can't believe you didn't tell me about it." He grinned. "It's just like you to keep all the fun for yourself!"

"You've been here for less than an hour," Arica warned him. "Just wait till you see your first pfiper."

"Pfiper? What is a pfiper?"

"Pfipers are little green snakes with wings," said Arica. "And poisonous, too. Trust me, you want to stay as far away from them as you can. I can't even begin to describe how sick you get when they bite you."

Later, as they were resting on a fallen tree trunk at the forest's edge, Nue filled them in on all the details of their quest.

"The man we are searching for is named Haggdorn," Nue explained as he stretched out with his back against the tree, then yawned. "At least, that's the information we received from one of our elves living in the South."

"You have elves passing you information?" asked Connor, grinning gleefully. "Like spies? This is getting more exciting by the minute!"

"Not so exciting if they get caught," Nue said dryly. "We've had people thrown in prison and just left there, or executed for crimes they didn't commit."

Connor gulped.

"During the Great War most of the elves fled from South Bundelag in fear of their lives," Nue continued. "Eventually slavery was outlawed, but the elves still living there work for next to nothing, under the most terrible conditions."

"Why don't they leave, then?" asked Connor, frowning in puzzlement.

"It is their home. It was long before the humans came."

Arica chewed thoughtfully on a blade of grass. Nearby, Wish munched happily, knee-deep in clover. "Does this Haggdorn have the *Book of Fairies*?" she asked.

"We think so," Nue said. "He is one of the richest merchants in South Bundelag, and he has several hobbies. One of them is raising fine horses and racing them. Another is collecting old and rare books. Our agent thinks some of the books he buys are stolen, but apparently this is not a problem for Haggdorn. If he wants an item, he gets it any way he can.

"The Fairy Queen instructed me to tell you that you are to *ask* Haggdorn for the book. I certainly don't think that he'll give it to you, and neither does the Queen, but you have to try. Then you will offer to buy it. The Fairy Queen has provided gold and jewels for this purpose.

"If this doesn't work, you'll be forced to steal the *Book of Fairies*. I know stealing is wrong, and both of you know it, too. But keep in mind, this book belongs to the fairies — and some of the secrets it contains would be dangerous if deciphered and used the wrong way. Don't think of it as stealing. Think of it as taking back what rightfully belongs to you and your people."

The idea of sneaking into South Bundelag to take a book from a very powerful man left a sick, twisty feeling in Arica's stomach. Wish, sensing her unhappiness, lowered her head and blew gently in her face.

"How will I recognize it when I find it?" she asked, then giggled as the warm air tickled her neck.

"The book is full of fairy magic," declared Nue. "The Fairy Queen believes you will have no trouble feeling its power."

"I hope that's true," said Arica, still feeling uneasy about the whole situation. She stood and hoisted her pack onto her shoulders. At least its weight made sense now: the lumpy, leather-covered package she'd seen Nue put inside must be the gold and jewels Grandmother had sent along.

"The Fairy Queen has asked me to travel throughout Bundelag, gathering elves for our army," said Nue. "But I will get you safely across the border, at least. For now we will follow the River of Songs as it continues south. When it turns and heads east, it becomes the dividing line between our country and the South. Any questions?"

"Not at the moment," said Arica, "but I'm sure I'll have at least a dozen when you're gone."

"Do we have to walk all the way?" asked Connor, scowling at the bundle Nue deposited at his feet. Connor had not brought a backpack to Bundelag, naturally. But Nue had kindly wrapped up a few necessities in an old shirt for him.

"That has all been taken care of by the Fairy Queen," the elf replied. "You will be provided with some transportation when we get to the border."

"Will Wish be coming with us?" asked Arica, but Nue was already heading out across the open plain, and either didn't hear her or chose not to answer.

A while later she heard the River of Songs.

The rivers of home trickled and gurgled pleasantly on their way, or roared and tumbled downward as rapids or falls. But the rivers of Bundelag did much more than this. The River of Songs called to Arica in a voice of harps and flutes that gradually deepened into one of oboes and horns.

The minutes passed; the singing and pulling grew stronger and stronger until she could no longer resist. Her pack dragged at her back. She could hardly keep herself from dashing off through the grass. The day was glorious and wonderful to see! Overhead, the sun blazed in a sky of cloudless joy. She would go to the river and fling herself into that lovely, life-giving water. She threw her unwanted pack to the ground and took off running.

Arica had taken only a few steps when something scooped her feet right out from under her and sent her sprawling, face first, into a patch of daisies.

Chapter 3

By the time Arica could breathe again she had recovered enough of her wits to realize what was going on. Nue had told her once that fairy folk were the only ones affected by the water in this way. He explained that somehow the pleasure centre of her brain was being stimulated, and that she *could* control the impulse if she worked hard enough at it. But the river had taken hold of her mind again.

She groaned and tried to sit up, and found herself tangled up with Connor. Her cousin rose to his knees, retrieved his glasses from the daisies, and set them back on his nose. "What did you do that for?" he squeaked.

Nue glowered.

"I've warned you more than once about what the river does to fairies," he scolded Arica. "Now look what happened! The boy almost followed you in. Luckily I saw this coming and prevented you from ending up neck-deep in the rapids, three kilometres downstream. Now get up, and let's get going. Remember, next time I won't be around to keep you on course!"

"Thanks, Nue," Arica said humbly, climbing to her feet. She obviously hadn't gotten any better at resisting the call of the river, or at least the first pull. Fortunately, the effect was fading to a tolerable level now.

Connor gazed longingly at the river as they trudged along beside it.

"The river sounds so . . . " he began.

"What?" asked Arica curiously.

"Cool," said Connor wistfully. He wiped the sweat from his face with his sleeve. "I thought we might get to swim."

"Nue is in a bit of a hurry today," Arica admitted. "But don't worry. He makes a lot of noise but he's soft underneath. He'll give us a break sooner or later."

Nue stopped in his tracks. "Soft underneath?" he practically wailed. "If you think that, you don't know me! Did I ever tell you about the time I single-handedly fought off a band of the most vicious trolls . . . "

Arica grinned to herself and stopped listening, but whatever the elf said, if it kept Connor happy for the next few hours, then it was worth it.

At suppertime they stopped at a place where a stretch of golden sand sloped gently to the shore. Arica sat at the water's edge and soaked her tired feet while Connor waded out to his knees with a fist-ful of rocks for skipping. Wish plunged in up to her chest and drank till Arica feared she might burst. The she bounced on past, soaking Arica in spray.

On shore, Nue built a small fire that he proudly lit with magic, and soon he had a variety of leaves and roots simmering in a pot. Arica didn't bother to ask what the little brown things were that he added at the last minute — some kind of high-protein river slug, no doubt. The soup tasted wonderful, although she and Connor picked out the boiled slugs and buried them in the sand when Nue wasn't looking. Soon they were all stretched out on the shore, relax-ing in the cool evening breeze.

They slept soundly in a lean-to of leaves and boughs — built by Nue and Connor after much hag-gling over how it should best be done — and rose early the next morning to resume their journey. In the late afternoon, Arica saw that the River of Songs would soon join up with another tributary and swerve east, forming the dividing line between North and South Bundelag.

"Look — we're almost there," she said to Nue, pointing. "Another few minutes of walking and we'll be across the border. But Grandmother said there would be patrols, and I don't seen anyone."

Nue bent over and plucked a blade of grass, then began to pick at his teeth with it. Weariness and worry made lines that ran across his skin like scars, and his tattered shirt and trousers were less than clean. But the light of good cheer shone brightly from his eyes, and his voice was filled with concern for only them.

"The patrols are there, all right. They're just hidden, watching for invading soldiers from the south. And the bridge is there too, but it's covered by your Grandmother's magic. As soon as we get close enough, we'll be able to see it."

"Sort of like the entrance from Earth?" Arica asked.

Nue nodded, then added: "And the answer to your other question is no."

It took Arica a moment to figure out what her other question was, and another to realize she wasn't going to accept the answer.

"Why can't Wish come with us?" she demanded. "We need her. She has the right to choose for herself! Let's ask her, and see what she says! Wish? Have you been listening?"

I cannot come, True Arica, said Wish. *Unicorns never travel to the country in the south. I was told this by my mother, Song.*

Arica whirled back toward Nue. He sighed, as though some great burden had fallen on him. "The Fairy Queen warned me you might react this way," he complained.

"Of course she did, because she knows how unfair this is!"

"No," Nue said, "unfair would be to ask Wish to come along. Unicorn horns are worth a fortune in the South. They are used by humans there to cure all kinds of ailments, from warts to scarlet fever. It is believed that a pinch of horn or hoof powder on food is an antidote for every kind of poison. It is believed that the touch of a unicorn's horn will make undrinkable water sweet and clean. It is believed that a hair from the mane or tail of a unicorn will bring good luck. Need I go on?"

Arica was too stunned to speak.

"You are right — the magic a unicorn can provide could be vital on this journey," Nue continued kindly. "But it would be too dangerous for Wish, I'm afraid. Even if she hid her horn with magic, a thing unicorns can easily do, she still looks and moves like a unicorn. The Fairy Queen thought about this long and hard, and came up with a solution. What we needed was a unicorn — with all the powers of its kind — that could pass for a horse. What was needed on this journey was a unicorn who had experience acting like a horse, a unicorn that had lived among humans."

Arica didn't like the direction this conversation was taking. In fact, something cold and lumpy was beginning to form in the pit of her stomach. Then out of the corner of her eye she saw a tall, grey form drift out from behind a hill and move slowly toward them. She didn't want to look. She couldn't look. But even as she prepared herself for the worst, she felt Shadow's mind reaching for her own.

The last time she had seen the shadow unicorn, they had battled one another upon the peak of Mine Mountain while lightning spit fire across the sky and thunder crashed around them. Without the help of the ogre eye — a gift from the father of Thilug, an ogre girl whose life she had saved — she might very well have lost her own life that night. But she had survived, and Shadow had disappeared — only to be brought back now by her own grandmother, the Fairy Queen of North Bundelag.

"Don't refuse to do this until you've heard the whole story," said Nue in a sombre, steady voice. "Shadow is sorry for what he did."

"But you don't understand, Nue," she whispered, as if doing so would keep the unicorn from overhearing. "He's not the right kind of sorry. He's sorry he couldn't get away with doing whatever he wanted. He's sorry he couldn't destroy the other unicorns without destroying all of Bundelag. But he's not the good kind of sorry, the kind that makes people — or unicorns — change."

Nue stared back into her eyes, but without his former confidence. "I know the Fairy Queen can't talk to unicorns the way you can," he said, just a little unsteadily, "but she is very wise and experienced. She and Shadow came to some kind of understanding, and she trusts him enough to send him on this journey. I think you should trust him, too."

The knots in Arica's stomach twisted a little tighter. She turned away from Nue's earnest stare. "I will travel with him because Grandmother wants me to, but I can't promise I will trust him," she said.

Connor, who had been standing some metres away, gazing at the river, suddenly started waving his arms and leaping through the grass. He had taken off his shoes, and Arica saw with some surprise that his feet were red and blistered. Bundelag had already taken a toll on him, and he had not complained.

"There's another unicorn coming!" he shouted eagerly. "Is it the transportation you talked about? Do we get to ride him?"

"Yes to the first question, maybe to the second," Nue responded, his face grim. "That will be up to the unicorn. Get your belongings gathered up and your shoes back on. I'll go with you to the bridge, but no farther. You will go to the city of Mulek, the place where Haggdorn lives. Go steadily south and you will hit a road. Follow that road east and you will come to Mulek. Here are the directions on how to find his house."

He thrust a scribbled note into her hand. Arica opened it and squinted down at it for a moment, then decided it was readable, though just barely.

Shadow neared them, then paused uncertainly and waited. Arica forced herself to look into his eyes, and her mind met his.

You cannot hide your feelings from me, True One, came his words inside her head. *You're worried. You don't want me here.*

He was thinner than when she had last seen him, and somehow more faded. It was like someone had wiped away much of the colour with a wet cloth, blurring the hard, rough edges. His coat was a lighter grey, and his horn, which had formerly been a deep, blood red, had dulled to the colour of dying leaves. She could count the ribs on his sides, and see shoulder and hip bones straining beneath the skin. It was clear that Shadow had suffered greatly, and for this she was sorry.

Something bumped against Arica's shoulder. She turned and wrapped one trembling arm around Wish's neck, leaning there until her pounding heart-beat slowed.

How are you, shadow unicorn? Wish asked the other animal.

Well enough, young Wish, replied Shadow, lowering his horn in greeting.

I will know if True Arica comes to harm.

I will not hurt her, Shadow said, and knowing unicorns cannot lie, Arica had to believe this, at least.

Nue helped them pack up their things, and then led them toward the riverbank. Shadow came last, trailing some distance behind. When Nue reached it he paused and waited until everyone caught up. He cleared his throat and twisted his hands in front of his stomach, then after a moment of courage-gathering, grabbed Arica and hugged her to his chest. Seeming embarrassed by his own boldness, he turned away and began fussing over their bags, making sure they had everything he thought they needed.

Arica kissed Wish's nose and rubbed behind her ears while Connor tried nervously to slip a bridle onto Shadow's lowered head. She felt a sudden surge of magic, and looked up just in time to see Shadow's horn disappear behind a spell, making him into what resembled a thin, rather long-legged horse. Connor gasped and jumped away.

Tell the boy to either lead me or ride me, Shadow said to her. *He must stop thinking* unicorn *and start thinking* horse.*

"He wants you to treat him like a horse," Arica

told Connor. Her cousin turned back toward the unicorn with renewed confidence and took a firm hold on the rein.

Ahead of them Nue took a step forward that Arica could have sworn would send him plunging into the rapids below. In an instant an old, rickety bridge shimmered into view beneath his foot and he beckoned for them to come.

One look at the structure made Arica wonder if it was any better than the empty air, but she'd just have to trust Grandmother and Nue on that one. She stepped carefully across, with no bad results, then paused and looked back. Now Connor had started across the bridge into South Bundelag, Shadow's hooves tapping out a rhythm against the weather-worn boards. The wind pushed gently against Arica's back, as if warning her away.

When they reached the other side, Connor and Shadow stopped. Connor assembled a verbal list of landmarks while Arica simply looked back. Nue and Wish stood side by side, gazing sorrowfully out across the river. The elf had taken a soiled handkerchief from his pocket and was mopping at his face. Wish's thoughts came clearly across the distance to Arica, filled with love and longing.

Be safe, True Arica, she said.

That night, as they camped in a gully beside a small spring that burst from beneath some boulders,

Grandfather paid them a visit.

Shadow, needing much less sleep than either Arica or Connor, told her he was going to scout around the campsite for danger. He promised to return before dawn. Arica and her cousin sat with their faces to the fire and watched the upward dancing of the flames, brought into being not by magic but by good, old-fashioned matches. Nue always talked about how she had her own magical skills, but apparently those skills didn't include bringing fire out of thin air. In her opinion, a bit of modern technology never hurt a situation. If she remembered

The wind pushed gently against Arica's back, as if warning her away.

correctly, she still had a flashlight crammed some-where in her bag.

Grandfather appeared directly above the fire without warning. Arica wasn't the least bit surprised. She'd been in Bundelag for two whole days already and he was past due for a visit. It was just unfortu-nate that she hadn't thought to warn Connor.

When the boy saw the figure of a full-grown man appear in mid-air right over their heads, he yelled and scooted backward, then scrambled to his feet. He didn't run away, though, which said something for his determination to be worthy of Bundelag.

Rather, he stood on shaking legs and stared up, his chest heaving. It didn't help matters that Grandfather's beard looked like a ball of grey wool chewed on by cats, or that his eyes glared fiercely beneath brows like bottlebrushes, or that his general shape recalled a large football tipped on end.

Grandfather had always been one for getting to the point.

"So you're after the *Book of Fairies*, are you?" he demanded, glaring down at her. "What do you think you're doing? Are you trying to get yourself killed?"

Chapter 4

"You're making me nervous, hanging over the heat like that," Arica said. "I'm afraid that if you stay up there too long you'll start to sizzle."

Grandfather scowled, then drifted away from the fire and down about a half a metre. He settled comfortably in the air, then peered down his nose at Connor, who had managed to slow his gasping to a mild wheeze.

"Who is this boy?" asked the old man as he searched through his pockets for his pipe.

"Grandfather, this is my cousin Connor. Our mothers are sisters, and we're in the same grade at school. Connor, this is my grandfather, Theodore

Warman." Then she added, for Connor's benefit: "He pops in and out like this all the time. You'll get used to it after a while."

Grandfather chuckled and gave up on the pipe. "Pleased to meet you, young man. You're a long way from home, aren't you? How did you get involved in this nasty business, anyway?"

Connor swallowed with some difficulty and, still sounding half-strangled, made his reply. "I fell through a crack in the kitchen floor."

"Of course. That's how everyone comes to Bundelag. You're a brave lad, I can tell. Frightened to death, but still standing firm. My dear granddaughter was wise to bring you along. It's always safer to have a partner on excursions such as these. Be careful, both of you, and beware of Haggdorn. He is a man blinded by his own greed."

Arica almost shook her head to clear her ears. Had she heard her grandfather correctly? The warning she had expected — he handed those out like candy — but his compliments were few and far between. And he seemed to have taken a liking to Connor, for some reason.

"Well, I have to go now," the old man said as he began to fade. "You know how it is."

"Yes, I know," she said. She was used to his coming and going. At least this time he hadn't disappeared in the middle of a sentence.

"May I ask you something, sir?" Connor called out to the fading figure of Grandfather. "I'm not trying to be rude or anything, but you're too cheery and colourful to be dead. Yet your body isn't very solid. Did some evil person put a spell on you?"

Grandfather, who had paled almost to invisibility, snapped back into focus like a light bulb blinking on. Then he swooped toward the boy and hovered above him, glaring down.

It was Connor's turn to pale. He pulled back with a new surge of alarm. "I didn't mean to pry into your personal life," he gasped. "I'm sorry if I offended you!"

Grandfather floated up again, looking much like a miniature thundercloud with lightning spitting around its edges.

"I accept your apology," Grandfather huffed. Then he was gone.

Connor looked like he'd just survived a personal-sized hurricane. "Oh, wow," was all he said. Arica figured that summed up the whole episode fairly well.

They spent the night sleeping restlessly beneath a thin blanket sent along by Nue, and woke up to grey skies, Shadow the unicorn peering down at them and raindrops dripping into their eyes.

After a miserable day of trudging through the wet clingy grass they arrived at the rim of a small town called Tak, on the east-west road Nue had described. Arica's relief at finally finding it didn't last for long, however. The road — hardly more than a wide trail, really — was thick with muck, and everywhere they stepped were deep ruts filled with muddy water. Shadow seemed able to sense and avoid them quite skilfully, but not so with her and Connor. They decided to ride.

This hardly increased their pace, however. For the next two days, the rain continued to drizzle down as they huddled on Shadow's bony, slippery back, his hooves sucking and slurping the mud below. Every time he tossed his head, his sodden mane whipped more water back into their faces. They slept little, and ate even less.

There was nothing to break the monotony of their endless ride. Even during those few brief moments when the rain let up enough to let the sun peek bravely through the clouds, they saw nothing but a wide, colourless plain that stretched out to meet the distant, empty horizon.

"They should have called this place Saskatchewan," Arica muttered, half to herself.

"The province of Saskatchewan at least has real roads, and wheat fields," Connor commented.

"Is that supposed to make me feel better?" she asked.

They arrived at the outskirts of Mulek in the

afternoon of the second day, too cold and sore to even feel relieved. Nue's directions sent them to the southwest corner of the city, and it was unlike any city she had ever seen before.

Arica imagined that this was how the cities of her own country might have looked two hundred years ago. There were no paved roads, power lines or cars of any kind. Instead, all she saw on the streets was a great variety of animals — mules, horses, goats and cows — being ridden or driven or led, pulling wagons or tied to posts, hooves deep in muck and manure.

The second street they took was clearly a market of some sort. Carts piled high with fruits and vegetables of every kind lined both sides of the road. The carcasses of pigs and birds and other animals she didn't recognize dangled from ropes or lay limply upon tables. The whole place swarmed with flies and wasps and humans, but that wasn't the worst of it.

No amount of explaining could have prepared her for the smell. The town reeked of sewer and sweat, old barnyards and meat left too long outdoors. And this was a cool day. She didn't want to think about how it would smell when the temperature hit 25 degrees.

They left the marketplace and headed down a residential street. The farther along they travelled, the larger were the houses and yards — until at last they arrived at the outskirts of the city once again.

An enormous house stood before them. It had three storeys, with half a dozen small black windows at the front, and was made of blocks of grey stone neatly laid. To the right of it were numerous oak trees that surrounded a well-tended pond. One tree was much larger than the rest and made Arica think of a mother hen spreading leafy wings to gather in her brood. Behind the house was a long, narrow red building that she guessed might be a stable. A white wooden fence enclosed the whole of it.

They slid off Shadow's back and stood staring up and shivering in their shoes, while Haggdorn the merchant's house loomed over them like a fortress carved in stone.

"I guess the direct approach would be best," Arica said as she swayed, weak with hunger and cold. "Should I knock, or do you want to?"

"Let's do this together," decided Connor.

They stumbled up the front walkway, half dragging, half supporting each other, and halted, staring at the door in shock and surprise. Carved into the massive oak planks was the body of a long, green snake. Two red eyes made of inlaid rubies glittered wickedly in its wooden face. The fangs that jutted from its open mouth were hunks of onyx, filed to points as sharp as needles.

"I'd hate to run into that in the dark," said Arica.

"It looks just like a giant pfiper."

"Something tells me we're dealing with a not-so-pleasant character," said Connor, shuddering. "Or at least one with very strange decorating tastes. If you want to change your mind and take us home, now would be a good time."

Arica grinned in spite of herself. "Not a chance," she said, and raised her knuckles to the wood.

At her third knock she started to get worried. The only thing worse than finding Haggdorn at home would be not finding him and having to wait around the city for hours or even days until he decided to turn up.

After the twelfth knock they were forced to conclude that no one was there, and climbed back on Shadow, their every muscle knotting in protest. The first inn they came to was too near the market for Arica's liking, but at this point, her discomfort won out over her unease. The innkeeper grinned at them through a curly red beard when Arica paid him with Grandmother's gold, and showed them to what he swore was his finest room. It was small and dark, with paint peeling off the walls; it had two narrow lumpy beds that creaked and sagged, and roaches that skittered into corners when Arica and Connor stepped inside. It smelled of mould and dirty socks, and the water in the wash basin was brown and cold.

But right then it was the most wonderful place Arica had ever seen.

Connor went to make sure Shadow was settled safely in his stall, then came stomping back in a while later, smelling like a barn. Arica dozed off three times during the meal of greasy chicken stew and stale bread brought by the innkeeper's plump, talkative wife; twice more as she was washing and brushing her teeth; and for the last time when she fell senseless into bed.

When Arica woke the next morning she was stiff and aching in every joint, but feeling almost alive again. After they had washed, she and Connor made their way to the kitchen where breakfast was being served.

They ate in the midst of a rabble of rowdy men — South Bundelag's version of truckers, Arica concluded, only with horses and wagons instead of semis. She guessed it didn't matter where you lived — goods still had to be hauled from here to there.

Two of the men made her particularly uneasy. They sat in a corner by themselves, and every once in a while one of them would glance in her and Connor's direction. The large one had black, greasy hair and a long beard that kept falling in his food. The thin one's bloodshot eyes had a hollow, haunted look, and his hand trembled when he raised his glass to drink.

She and Connor ate as quickly as they could, paid for their breakfast with another of Grandmother's coins, and rose from their table. They had barely stepped outside when they were attacked from behind.

The thin man grabbed Arica and pulled her against him. He reeked of body odour and beer, but his arms were like steel wires holding her down. The hairy one got Connor in a neck lock and started to squeeze. The boy let out a strangled scream and aimed a vicious kick at the man's shin. The man swore and tightened his hold even more, choking off Connor's air.

In the meantime, Arica struggled wildly and managed to free enough of an arm to elbow the thin one in the ribs. He flung her down, knocking the breath completely out of her, and tore the pack from her back.

Connor landed beside her, gasping for air. She heard the clatter of objects being dumped upon the ground and tried to rise. By the time she and Connor had recovered enough to stand, the thieves had made off with their ransom for the *Book of Fairies*.

Arica sat down upon the wet, cold ground amid her scattered belongings, put her face into her hands and squeezed her eyes shut to keep the tears from coming. Connor sank down in the mud beside her and patted her arm in an awkward, boyish way. After

The thin man grabbed Arica and pulled her against him.

a few sniffs she looked up at him and wiped her hands across her face.

"What do we do now?" he asked.

"The most important thing is not to give up," she said as she gathered her things and stuffed them angrily into her bag. She couldn't help but notice that Connor's bundle hadn't been touched. The thieves had certainly known where to look. Was it the innkeeper who had tipped them off, or his chubby, chatty wife? It was pointless to confront them. Likely she would never know. She slung her pack back over her shoulder and headed for Shadow's stall.

While Connor struggled to pull Shadow's bridle over a horn he couldn't see, despair grew inside Arica like a knot in her stomach that twisted tighter and tighter. Somehow, they had to find a man who wasn't home, buy back a book with money they didn't have, then get back to North Bundelag on a horse that wasn't a horse and that couldn't be trusted. How could things get any crazier than that?

She was a grim, silent girl when she and her two travelling companions arrived back at Haggdorn's front door.

This time their knocking was answered. The man at the door made Arica think of King Henry VIII. She had never seen King Henry VIII, of course, but she'd seen a famous picture of him, and this was it.

Not the clothes, for the man was dressed in a nineteenth-century style, with a short waistcoat, a brown coat with tails, and long, tight trousers. Rather, it was his enormous belly, his full red cheeks, his double chin, and the way he looked down his long, arrogant nose at her with something much like pity.

"Are you Mr. Haggdorn?" Arica asked boldly and a little too loudly, as she tried to keep her voice from shaking.

Haggdorn nodded coolly, and stepped aside.

The man who stood behind him in the doorway was tall, handsome and dark-haired. The eyes that looked into hers had looked there many times before, and the voice that sounded in her ears was one she knew all too well.

"Hello, dear Niece," said the Fairy Queen's eldest son Raden, Arica's own uncle, and her sworn enemy. "Come in. We've been expecting you."

Chapter 5

"How did you know we were coming?" Arica asked as Raden escorted them into the huge front hallway. A high, beamed ceiling peaked above their heads. To their right, stairs of carved oak curved upward to a second floor. All along one wall oil lamps flickered, adding their glow to the feeble light cast by the high, narrow windows. Tapestries of blue and green adorned the walls. Rugs of the same colours lay scattered over wooden floors. Chairs, sofas and tables that would have made an antique-furniture lover weep graced the room with elegance.

"I have my ways," Raden said as he closed the door behind them. But just before it swung shut, he glanced past her and Connor and saw Shadow standing by the gate.

"I see you've brought along the shadow unicorn — disguised as a horse," he said, shaking his head in amusement. "That was a foolish thing to do. Sooner or later the word will get out that there's a unicorn here. The minute he steps off this property, he'll have all the riffraff in Mulek City trying to hunt him down."

"A unicorn?" asked Haggdorn, raising one elegant brow, his eyes lighting with interest. He turned to Raden. "What a rare privilege. I have always wanted to see one. I'll go make sure that he's fed and cared for properly." He slipped quickly from the room.

Raden's dark eyes rested coldly upon Connor. "Who is this?" he said, his gaze sliding scornfully over the boy's thin body. "What backwater hole did you drag him out of?"

Arica glared back, her anger making her bold. "You answer my question first," she retorted. "Then maybe I'll answer yours."

Her uncle studied her face thoughtfully for one long moment, then burst into harsh, unpleasant laughter. It was a sound that reminded Arica of rocks thunking on old tin cans.

"My foolish mother, the Fairy Queen, has spies lurking about this fine country, pretending to be the servants of innocent, decent folk like my kind host

Haggdorn. Luckily for him, upon my arrival in Mulek I recognized his stable boy as a close friend of the Fairy Queen's. The plot was exposed, and the thieving elf was stopped from doing any more damage."

"Where is this elf now?" asked Arica, but the only reply she got was a scowl. "I answered your question, now you answer mine," Raden demanded.

"All right," she said, trying not to grind her teeth in frustration. "This is Connor, my cousin from home. He came here by accident. He's my friend."

Raden's dark brows soared. "A human followed you through the crack? How interesting. And what does my dear mother have to say about that?"

Arica didn't think it was any of his business, and would have told him so, too, but the next moment Haggdorn stepped quietly back into the room. It surprised her that a man of his height and girth could move so lightly on his feet.

"The unicorn is taken care of," the large man announced, "though I saw no horn, and his owner has not groomed or fed him properly for some time." He threw Arica a horse-lover's look of disapproval. "My elf is taking care of that now."

"Trust me — the animal is a unicorn," Raden replied. "And he has no owner. The only tending and feeding he gets is from himself. I know you're fascinated by the creature, but trust me, he's as wild as a mountain cat and twice as unpredictable. Your elf will be lucky if he doesn't lose a finger or two. Forget the animal for now. We have business to conclude. Shall we go?"

Haggdorn nodded, and as the two men turned away, he spoke to Arica and Connor over his shoulder.

"Go up the stairs. The first and second doors on the right are your rooms. You are my guests so make yourselves at home. You may wash and rest, and look around if you like. There is food in the kitchen if you cannot wait for dinner at six o'clock. Join me then, in the dining hall." Then the door clicked shut behind them.

Connor stared in surprise at the closed door, then at Arica.

"Why didn't you ask Haggdorn about the *Book of Fairies*?" he asked. "Do you think he even has it?"

"I'm sure he does," Arica said as she started for the stairs. "And I think that reference to 'business' was my dear uncle's opening move in a little bidding game. I should have realized when Grandmother exiled Raden that he'd end up where he could cause the most trouble. In fact, I wouldn't be surprised if he's using Haggdorn for some slimy purpose of his own. That's how he operates. You can be sure he dragged every morsel of information he could from that poor elf spy before he was through with him."

"Do you think the elf is still alive?" asked her cousin, pausing in front of the first bedroom door.

"I sure hope so," said Arica grimly, and let herself in.

The room was a pleasant contrast to the inn of the night before. It was spotlessly clean, and contained one bed piled high with quilts and cushions. On the floor beside the bed lay the pelt of some poor animal — possibly a bear. One small window let in enough light to turn the hanging tapestry into a shimmer of gold and green. A nightstand with a wash basin, a towel and a pitcher of water filled up one corner. In the other stood an old wooden dresser.

Arica placed her bag on top of the dresser and sat down uneasily on the edge of the bed. It wouldn't do to get too comfortable here. Raden was up to something, of that she was certain. It was one of those things you could count on, like the sun coming up every morning, or schoolwork, or your feet getting too big for your shoes.

After a while she lay down on the cushions, deciding that a brief rest probably wouldn't hurt, as long as she didn't close her eyes . . .

She woke up to the sound of frantic thumping just outside her room. She rolled off the pillows, staggered sleepily to the door and yanked it open. Before her stood Connor, his hand raised for another volley of pounding. He grinned at her and stepped quickly inside, pulling the door shut behind him.

"What is it?" she said, trying to rub the fuzzy feeling out of her eyes.

"I came by a couple of hours ago," he explained in a rush. "You were so quiet I thought you must be sleeping, so I went exploring without you."

"Exploring?" She was having trouble getting her brain to make the right connections. Oh, yes. They were here at the rich merchant's house. So far he was treating them well. He had even given them the freedom to look around.

"There are some things I want to show you," her cousin continued, and grabbed her arm.

"In that case, I hope our first stop will be the kitchen," she said, awakening enough to notice the hollow pain in her stomach. "I don't know about you, but I'm starved."

After a late lunch of roast venison sandwiches, pickles and tomatoes, cheese and apples, and clear, icy water, Connor led her out of the house through the back door. They went past a grove of trees surrounding a small pond, then over a fence and into a long red building.

Once inside, Arica saw that stalls ran along both sides of the structure from one end to the other. At least half of them held horses. A boy came toward them, leading a black mare. He passed by and glanced at them uneasily from the corners of his eyes. Arica noticed a flash of green, and glimpsed a pair of sharp-tipped ears peeking up through yellow hair.

At the far end of the stable they found Shadow's stall. Arica unlatched the door and stepped inside. The unicorn waited for her with his head lowered. She brushed the forelock from his eyes and touched his now-visible horn. It shone rusty-red in the dim stable light, and Shadow's dark magic pricked her fingertips and tingled up her arm.

"Are you sure it's wise to leave your horn showing like that?" she asked with some concern.

No one would dare harm me while I'm under Haggdorn's protection, Shadow assured her. *If it makes you feel any better, I'll hide it again when I leave the stable, although I don't know why you'd even care."

Arica let that one pass. "How have they treated you?" she asked, noting the manger overflowing with fresh hay and the bucket of clean water by his feet.

Haggdorn is good to his animals, replied the unicorn, *but the elves in his employ seem nervous.*

Connor's head popped around the corner of the open doorway. "Don't you think this place is incredible?" he cried. "There must be a hundred horses here! They're a breed I don't recognize — tall, like thoroughbreds — but even faster. You should see them run!"

Arica stepped out of Shadow's stall and closed the

door behind her, only half listening to Connor's excited babble. "When Grandmother exiled Uncle Raden from the North," she thought aloud, "the South was the only place he could go. But why did he come to the city of Mulek? And why to the house of Haggdorn? Obviously he found out about the *Book of Fairies*. My guess is he wants to keep Grandmother from getting it."

Shadow peered out at her over the door. *This is true,* he said. *The fairy Raden wants to keep the book for himself.*

Icy fingers closed in on Arica's heart. The spells alone, in Raden's hands . . . she couldn't bear thinking about the damage he could do. But there was more. "Grandmother thinks the book might help us to find the lost fairies. Could he want it for the same reason? If he found them, how would that benefit him? Maybe he's looking for someone to side with him against Grandmother."

She met Shadow's dark, unblinking stare. "Is this what he has planned?" she asked. "Do you know something I don't?"

I know that I am very tired, the unicorn replied, and withdrew into his stall.

She wanted to call him back and make him talk some more, but she knew him well enough to realize she had to let him be. He would only tell her what he wanted to, and only when he was ready. Or maybe he wouldn't tell her anything at all. With a heavy heart, she turned back to Connor.

"Come," her cousin said, taking her arm. "I want to show you the library."

Arica was not prepared her for what she saw. She knew Haggdorn collected books, but judging by their sheer number, he must have brought them in by horse and wagon. The room was as large as her grade five classroom back home, and twice its height. Floor to ceiling shelves covered all four walls, and each shelf was stuffed to overflowing. Cabinets stood back to back in the centre of the room, also filled to capacity. There were books stacked on tables, piled in corners, and heaped in chairs. She had never seen so many books in all her life.

Arica walked carefully around the room, finding it difficult to even take a step without treading on one volume or another. At last she found a bare stool and sank down on it.

"You don't have to say it," said Connor from somewhere among the books. "A needle in a haystack."

Arica lifted her head with a sudden thought, her heart thudding with hope. "Nue said I would be able to feel the book's power. Don't talk, Connor. Give me a minute." She stood and moved carefully up and down the aisles. Now was the time to discover the special magic Nue had always said she had. Up and down the rows she went, reaching and feeling for something that was more than just an ordinary book.

In a few minutes she became aware of someone shaking her roughly by the shoulders. Gradually Connor's frowning face came into focus.

"We've got to get out of here!" he hissed. "It's six o'clock. Haggdorn and Raden are expecting us for dinner."

What had seemed to her like minutes of looking had, in reality, taken nearly an hour. She was no expert in fairy magic, but she was pretty sure the book wasn't in this room.

Dinner turned out to be a grand affair, fitting of Haggdorn's lofty place in South Bundelag society. They sat at a long wooden table that reminded Arica a little of the one in the Fairy Queen's castle, though this one was not as fine, or magical. Before them were placed dishes piled high with roasted chicken, sweet potatoes and corn, bread still steaming from the oven, butter and honey, and pitchers of purple grape juice tinkling with ice. They were served by an old elf woman with pale, weary eyes. They talked little. Afterward Haggdorn smoked, while Raden gazed at them mockingly over the rim of his silver goblet.

"Did you find what you were looking for?" he asked.

. . . *Raden gazed at them mockingly over the rim of his goblet.*

Connor's ears went red and his chin burrowed down into his collar. Arica fared better, being more used to her uncle Raden's bluntness. Her uncle had brought things out into the open. Now was the time for her to make her move.

"No, as a matter of fact we didn't," she replied smoothly. "But this matter has nothing to do with you, dear uncle." She turned and boldly addressed their host. "Mr. Haggdorn, we would like to thank you for your kindness and hospitality. You must know that we have come on behalf of the Fairy Queen of North Bundelag in search of the *Book of Fairies*. It is a priceless record belonging to the fairy people, and it has been lost for over four hundred years. We are aware that you now own this valuable book. If you can't afford to give it to us, I can offer you a fair price in the queen's gold and jewels."

Raden's laughter barked like angry dogs. "What gold and jewels?" he sneered. "You've only been in Mulek for a day and a half, and you've already managed to get them stolen!"

Arica fixed him with a daggers-of-ice stare. "How would you know that, Uncle Raden?" she said.

Haggdorn nodded thoughtfully. His face was, as always, polite and unreadable. "I regret that your journey to my city has been for nothing," he said in his lacklustre way of speaking. "I have already accepted an offer for the *Book of Fairies*. I must admit" — here his eyebrows rose a fraction — "I am a trifle puzzled, as the offer seems to be on the same authority as yours. It is from your uncle, son of the Fairy Queen, and heir, I understand, to the throne of North Bundelag. So you see, I *am* returning the book to its rightful owner."

Raden smiled at her with the hard glitter of victory in his eyes. Arica sat, stunned, as Haggdorn gestured with his hand. The elf woman emerged from the shadows and whisked their plates away.

"Dessert will be served shortly," Haggdorn said, the perfect host. "I'm sure you'll enjoy the fruit from my garden, which I have instructed should be served with pudding and cream."

"Will you please excuse me, Mr. Haggdorn?" Arica said through the roaring in her ears and the pounding of her heart. "I don't feel hungry any more."

His brow furrowed with concern. "I'm sorry to hear that," he said. "I trust you will stay the night. Your beds are made and waiting. Breakfast will be served whenever you want it."

"Thank you," she managed to say. She stood and walked, outwardly calm, to the door. Once in the hall, she took off running as fast as her legs would go.

Chapter 6

Connor slipped quietly into Arica's room just before midnight. When she heard the door creak open she turned toward the sound, as wide awake now as when she had climbed into bed hours before.

"I have one more place to show you," he whispered as he tiptoed across the floor. He grinned, clearly pleased with himself. "I think I might have found where your grandmother's spy is being kept."

Light from Bundelag's two moons fell in through the overhead window, setting his face aglow and sparkling in his hair like diamond dust. Arica tossed her covers aside and rose, still fully clothed, to pull on her shoes.

"We might as well try to save him," Arica whispered back. "We've accomplished nothing else here. What do we have to lose?"

Later she would remember those casually spoken words and realize how much they really did have left to lose. But at that moment, with Grandmother's gold and jewels taken and the *Book of Fairies* practically in Raden's hands, things seemed pretty hopeless.

Halfway to the door, she paused and turned back. It was always better to be prepared; she would definitely need the flashlight, and perhaps even the sword. She grabbed them both and headed after Connor.

Along the upstairs hallway they tiptoed, then down the great, curved staircase to the floor below. They sped through several rooms and into the kitchen, where Connor pointed out a narrow door, half hidden behind a cupboard. Her cousin had indeed done some serious exploring.

This door took them down a set of twisting stone stairs that descended into a pool of blackness too thick for her eyes to penetrate.

"Time for the flashlight," he said, and she snapped it on. They continued downward for what seemed to Arica like a terrible length of time. The air around them grew heavier and damper with each step, and the way steeper. At last they hit bottom — and their feet nearly slid out from under them. The floor of the underground tunnel was made of stones like greased tiles, and on the walls, water seeped through patches of slug-grey fungus. Arica shivered and took hold of Connor's arm.

"I didn't have a flashlight the first time," he explained, "so I didn't make it to the bottom. This is an excellent place to hide someone, don't you think? It reminds me of a creepy old dungeon in some cheesy horror movie. I'm betting there's a room at the end of this tunnel with a door and a lock."

As it turned out, there were three rooms and three doors, but only one lock. Through the iron-barred window of the one closed door they saw someone curled up on the floor sleeping. Then that someone raised his head and they saw it was an elf. The elf had matted, dingy hair that had probably once been golden. His clothing hung from his limbs like rags, and his green eyes stared bleakly up at them from a face streaked with mud and slime.

The elf recognized Arica at almost the same instant that she knew him. "Perye!" she said, through a sudden lump in her throat that nearly choked her. This was Perye, Nue's nephew, her travelling companion during her first trip to the land of Bundelag. There were few friends closer to her or to the Fairy Queen than this one. It would have broken Grandmother's heart to see Perye suffering like this, just as it was breaking hers. "We have to get him out," she said fiercely.

"I can pick the lock," said Connor. "Just let me find something long and sharp." He started to pull things from the pockets of his jeans.

Perye rose and tottered toward them. He pressed his pale face up to the door's one small window. Grimy, trembling fingers reached through the bars toward her. Arica grasped them with her own.

"Hold on, Perye," she said. "We'll break down the door if we have to."

Out from Connor's pockets came a spool of thread, two safety pins, a half-used package of spearmint gum, three loonies and a quarter, a rusty nail, a wad of duct tape and a ballpoint pen. He shoved everything back but the nail, held it up and studied it for a moment, then began jabbing it into the lock.

"Get out of here before they catch you," gasped Perye. His voice was weak and shaky.

"Not without you," she insisted. Connor's nail rattled in the lock, but the door held firm.

"Haggdorn carries a special key for this lock," Perye rasped, nearly desperate now. "You'll never get it open with anything else." He paused. "What you really need is a unicorn," he added, and laughed weakly at his own joke. "Did you happen to bring one along, unicorn-girl?"

A unicorn? Magic? That was it! Shadow was too far away for her to draw on his power. But she *had* brought her father's sword.

"Stand back," she said to Connor. "There's a faster way!" And she unhooked the weapon from her belt.

It was a small sword, forged of finest steel, made with spell and song. With it in her hand, she had come as close as ever to having magic of her own. She felt the power as it tingled up her arm and spread like fire across her skin. Pointing the weapon toward the door, she sent it streaking toward the lock.

She felt the power as it tingled up her arm and spread like fire across her skin.

There was a sound like a bullet striking stone, a hot hissing sound, and then the door swung open, all melted metal and charred wood. Connor clapped his hands and whooped. Perye swayed weakly in the doorway and stared at something beyond her left shoulder.

"My, my," came a mocking voice from behind them. "Wasn't that a delightful little display! It was most entertaining, I must say, though somewhat hard on the ears. But I guess no escape attempt is ever perfect."

Arica knew before she turned around who the

owner of that awful voice was. Unfortunately, there was no way to avoid the consequences of getting caught in the act.

Haggdorn stood several metres away, holding a torch and gazing with mild concern at the shattered, smoking door. At his side was Raden, eyes glittering like cold pebbles in the torch's yellow glare. He remained there only a moment, then strode forward and yanked the sword and the flashlight from her hands.

"As usual, my dear niece is in the thick of the trouble," he said to Haggdorn. "It seems that a little lesson needs to be taught here. Don't you agree?"

The other man shrugged. "This looks like a family matter," he said. "Do as you please." And he walked away.

"Get in there," Raden commanded, pushing her and Connor toward one of the other rooms. "You too, elf," he said to Perye, and shoved them all inside. Then the door clanged shut, leaving them all in darkness.

It was difficult for Arica to tell how long they stayed locked inside their prison, but it seemed like time slowed to a turtle's crawl. None of them had a wristwatch and it was just as well. Raden likely would have taken those, too, and sold them to Haggdorn — no doubt he would find such an Earth treasure fascinating.

There were no windows except for the one on the door, but that did them no good as the tunnel wasn't lighted. When Grandfather dropped in for another one of his surprise visits, it was lucky that his body brought its own light along with it, or they wouldn't have seen much of him, or he of them. They were hungry and thirsty. Perye, already weakened, lay hardly breathing, his head in Arica's lap. Connor had exhausted himself pacing back and forth in an attempt to avoid the wetness, the cold, the bugs and the strange scurrying and scratching noises (rats, Arica assumed). At last, he had given up and fallen asleep.

Grandfather drifted in through the window in the door and settled half a metre off the floor. The warm white glow from his body spread cheerfully across the room and Arica's eyes gradually adjusted to the light. She pretended not to see a furry creature with four feet and a tail scurry to one corner while she brushed a large black spider off her arm and another from her knee. She had to clamp her jaws to keep from screaming out loud.

"How are you, Grandfather?" she asked at last, and then was surprised at how weak and quavery her own voice sounded.

"Clearly much better than you," he said sadly, pulling a bottle of something from his pocket. It was clean, sweet water, and he made her drink her fill.

He offered the bottle to Connor, now awake and blinking, then dribbled some of the liquid between Perye's cracked and swollen lips. After that he dug out a couple of sandwiches. As they chewed he watched silently, pulled a handkerchief from his pocket and dabbed at his eyes.

"Things will get better for you soon," he said with real pain in his voice. "Trust me. Just hold on a little longer."

"That's fine for you to say!" Connor piped up through a mouthful of cheese and ham. "You can just float out through a wall any time you want!"

Grandfather studied the boy's face unhappily for one long moment. Arica had to admit the sight of Connor did tend to make one feel bad. Wet, dirt-smeared and cold, he shivered against the dank, wet wall, his arms as thin and white as bones. She didn't figure she looked much better, and they all knew how poorly Perye was doing.

Grandfather had already started to fade away, taking all that wonderful light with him. But just before he disappeared altogether, his voice drifted back to them with a sound like wind through grass.

"You were right about me, lad," he said with great sadness. "I am alive — barely. I am under a terrible spell, cast by an old enemy. The spell turned me into a living ghost. During my visible times, I have only enough magic to conjure up bits of food, or small magical tools, or a few swallows of water. Only my wife, the Fairy Queen — and now you and my granddaughter — know this awful secret."

And he was gone.

"Oh, wow," said Connor for the second time.

Arica shook her head in amazement. So Grandfather was under a spell, was he? How had Connor managed to guess so quickly, when she had been puzzling over it since her first trip to Bundelag? The longer she spent with her cousin, the more she realized how much more there was to him than it appeared.

A while later Perye stirred in her arms and spoke. "I had the strangest dream," he said, his voice hardly stronger than a whisper.

"What was it?" Arica asked as her heart flooded with relief. Perhaps if she kept him talking, he wouldn't get around to dying.

"I dreamed about an old man . . . here in the room . . . he seemed to float in mid-air."

"Actually, it wasn't a dream," Connor informed the elf. "But don't ask us to explain. It's a long story."

"I don't think — " Perye started to say, but a sudden sound in the darkness drew their attention away from all thoughts of strange visitors, in the air or otherwise. It was the sound of a key being inserted in a lock.

Chapter 7

They sat and stared in the direction of the sound, hardly daring to breathe. Several thoughts flashed through Arica's mind, fuelled by hope. Was it Haggdorn, remembering his reputation as a good host, here to bring them food and warm, dry blankets? Had Raden decided to set them free? Or had the Fairy Queen arrived to rescue them and take the *Book of Fairies* home?

The door creaked open to reveal two slender female figures standing in a blaze of yellow torchlight. Arica covered her eyes, then peeked out between her fingers while her eyes adjusted to the glare.

She recognized the first elf as the old woman who had served their dinner the evening before. It took her a moment longer with the other, simply because it had been so long — and hers was the last face Arica expected to see here.

"Drusa!" croaked Perye, and struggled to rise.

It was Drusa, sister of Perye — the first person to show kindness to Arica when she was a prisoner in Raden's mine, those many months ago. Because of Drusa, Perye had finally come to trust Arica. With the help of the other elves and some unicorns, Perye and Drusa had freed themselves and the other slaves.

Drusa leaped into the room and threw her arms around her brother, who struggled to his knees. The force of her embrace sent them both toppling backward into the mud and slime, but neither seemed to care much. All that came from the tangled heap on the floor were peals of near-hysterical laughter.

The old elf woman barely glanced at them. "My master and his guest will not be gone for long," she told Arica and Connor in a voice tight with fear. "You must hurry and leave this city. I need to return the key to my master's room. Close the door behind you, and it will take longer for them to discover that you're missing."

She passed her torch to Arica and turned to go.

"Thank you for taking such a great risk for us," Arica said, but the woman had already slipped away.

Now there was only the long, dark tunnel, and the flickering light of the torch in Arica's trembling hand.

Drusa and Perye had managed to gather themselves up off the floor, Perye hooking one arm around his sister's neck as she rose. Connor grabbed the elf's other arm and draped it over his own shoulder. With Arica in the lead, they made their way through the tunnel and back up the narrow stairway.

"The Fairy Queen asked us to live in Mulek and send back information," Drusa explained as they climbed. "Perye was the one who first discovered the *Book of Fairies*, and he immediately passed on the information to our contact. I didn't hear from Perye for a long time after that. I became worried and came to find out what was wrong. I discovered Raden was here, and since he knows Perye, that meant our cover was blown. I hid out for a few days, making a rescue plan. You know the rest. You've attracted a lot of unwanted attention by coming here, though. There's talk all over town about two children and a unicorn."

"We didn't intend for that to happen," admitted Arica, "but we didn't know Raden was here. He recognized Shadow as soon as he saw him, even without the horn."

They arrived at the top of the stairs and stepped into the warm, dry kitchen. The evening sunlight seeped through the white gauze curtains in pools of pink and gold, and Arica could hardly believe such beauty could exist in the same place as the ugliness in the cellar.

She set the torch in an empty bracket on the wall. "No need for that any more," she said as she paused and gazed out the window at the dazzle of blue and green. It seemed like another world.

"Hurry up," Drusa called to her. "There'll be time for sightseeing later!"

They left the house through one of the back doors and headed into the grove of oak trees. Arica couldn't help but notice the little blue birds that chirped in the treetops, and the way the sunlight caught their wings.

"I've got a horse hidden in the trees," the elf girl informed them as they went. "There's water and food in the saddlebags. When you're ready, Perye and I will take the horse and return to North Bundelag. You and Connor should get the unicorn and follow as soon as you can. I hate to say this, but there's nothing more we can do here. The mission is over."

Arica shook her head. "The *Book of Fairies* is too important — and I can't leave without my father's sword."

Drusa frowned. "It's too dangerous. The Fairy Queen will have to send someone to try again later."

"There will be no later! Raden has already struck a deal with Haggdorn. We must find the book before Raden disappears with it!"

Drusa's reply was interrupted at that moment by Perye. The pace had become too much for the elf, and he stumbled, too sick and weak from hunger and days of lying on cold floors to go on. Arica waited with him beneath the trunk of the biggest oak tree, while Connor and Drusa went to fetch the horse and the food and water.

While they waited the sun sank low. It spilled across the pond in waves of fire that blazed briefly across its surface and were gone. A warm breeze plucked at their hair and brushed their skin like fingers gloved in silk.

Arica sat with her back against the oak tree and closed her eyes. Something seemed to tug at her, drawing her closer and closer still. She stood and turned, then wrapped her arms around its ancient, gnarled trunk and breathed in the scent of leaves, and of roots sunk deeply into earth. Bubbles of warmth tingled over her skin and travelled down the entire length of her body. She clung there, not wanting the feeling ever to end.

After a while she opened her eyes to see Connor and Drusa scowling at her impatiently. "This isn't the time for hugging trees," Drusa said. "You have to eat."

There was only water, hard cheese and the dried fruit and nut mixture all elves seemed to carry around with them. When they were done, they spent a minute or so hugging each other goodbye. Then Arica and Connor helped boost Perye onto the elf-sized brown horse that waited so patiently, munching happily on grass. Drusa sat behind Perye, supporting his tired slump.

"Be careful," she said, gazing down on Arica with worry written plainly on her face. "We'll see you soon in North Bundelag."

"Thank you, once again, for saving my life," said Perye, reaching down to squeeze her hand. "You're beginning to make a habit of it."

She laughed. "A bit like the habit you have of saving mine."

Then the elves rode away in a flurry of waves and blown kisses, leaving Arica feeling strangely empty and alone.

"Somehow, things didn't seem quite so bad with them around," sighed Connor, putting her feelings into words.

"You won't find more loyal friends anywhere," Arica said.

As they made their way back through the trees, Arica felt the heavy touch of nightfall closing in around them. Good. Nightfall would give Drusa and Perye a better chance to get away without being seen, and it lessened the likelihood of her and Connor getting caught. Maybe their luck was finally taking a turn for the better.

Somewhere above their heads an owl hooted. One of the moons slid out briefly from beneath a gauzy cloud, then disappeared again. Trees groped skyward with twisted, broken arms. By their feet, crickets chirped and scurried for cover.

Inside Haggdorn's house, lanterns blazed. Either Haggdorn and Raden were home, or the housekeeper was going from room to room preparing for her master's return. Arica hoped it was the latter.

"I've thought this over very carefully, and here's what I've come up with," Arica told her cousin. "To save time, I think we should split up. You search for the sword while I go back to the library and look around one more time for the *Book of Fairies*. There were a couple of places I missed the first time. I left a torch on the wall inside the kitchen. Take it — I'll only have one room to search. We'll meet back at the kitchen in an hour. Got it?"

She thought for a moment that his cheeks grew pale beneath the moonlight, and that a trace of fear glinted in his eyes. But perhaps this was only a trick of the shadows, for the next moment he smiled bravely, raised his chin and squared his bony shoulders, and said in a voice that hardly squeaked at all, "Good luck to you, then."

Chapter 8

They entered the house through the same door they had so recently come out of. Arica raised her finger to her lips and they stood for a moment by the kitchen cupboard, waiting and listening. When all seemed clear, they started through the house.

It took Arica no time at all to reach the library, which was lit, to her relief, by one small lantern glowing above the door. Arica took it down and held it above her head as she made her way up and down the rows of books. She couldn't help but shiver a time or two, for in the half-darkness her own long-limbed shadow stalked her like a silent, stealthy ghost.

Her third time past the large table in the middle of the room, she spotted the book. It lay half hidden under a copy of *The Big Book of Medicinal Herbs*. Was that why she had missed it? Or had Raden cloaked it with a spell, so that her first search would be fruitless? She pulled out the book and studied it for one long moment.

It was exactly how she had imagined the *Book of Fairies* would be: covered with soft black leather, the title painted in gold letters across the front. Inside, the pages were yellowed with age and crackled softly when she turned them. It seemed handwritten, in a black, spider-web-thin scrawl. She saw recipes where she didn't recognize a single ingredient, peculiar laws that had no meaning, and magic spells containing words she had no idea how to say.

At the back of the book she found the fairies' names. The list ran on for several pages. Her heart ached for all the lost fairies. Near the end, she found her own name, as well as that of her Uncle Raden, her father, and of course her grandmother, the Fairy Queen of North Bundelag.

She closed the book and tucked it under her shirt. Hardly daring to believe her good fortune, she made her way back down the aisles of shelves, returned the lantern to its peg, and left the library. She closed the door behind her as she went out.

The house remained silent as she hurried from room to room. Now that she had actually found what she was looking for, the stress of these last few days caught up with her in a single rush. Her stomach knotted sickly beneath her ribs. Her knees wobbled and her teeth chattered. She arrived at the kitchen, praying that Connor had found the sword, hoping they could finally leave this house and this country forever.

Arica burst into the kitchen, and what she saw brought her to a sudden jerking halt as her heart leaped into her throat.

The good part was that Connor had found the sword, her pack and his own little bundle, and was waiting by the cupboard clutching all of these in his arms. The bad part was that Haggdorn and Raden stood beside him.

"Why, there you are," said Raden when he saw her. "Haven't you been a busy little girl!"

There was nothing she could say that wouldn't make things worse than ever, so she settled for not speaking at all. Connor cleared his throat nervously, sounding a bit like he was strangling on his own air. Haggdorn smiled, with chilling good cheer.

"I see you've escaped from the cellar," he said in that deadpan way he had of speaking. "I also must assume, by the way you came flying through the doorway just now, looking so pleased with yourself, that you've found the *Book of Fairies*. I must say, you are a rather . . . *active* guest."

"No, she didn't go there or find anything," said Connor, pleading at her with his eyes. "Tell them, Arica!"

Raden's laughter rattled like pebbles on tin. "Go ahead, Haggdorn — ask her. She won't lie. She's a favourite with the unicorns, and apparently they are creatures of truth."

Haggdorn's brows arched gracefully upward. One finger skimmed thoughtfully across his smooth-shaven double chin. "More and more interesting," he said. "Is it true, girl? Do you have the *Book of Fairies?*"

"Yes," said Arica miserably, and produced the book from beneath her shirt. Connor made a sound like someone trying unsuccessfully to breathe under water.

"It is a difficult position I find myself in," their host said, beginning to pace back and forth across the room. "I received guests into my home with gracious good will. I fed them, provided beds for the night and saw to their every need. And how was I repaid? With meddling and thievery. I feel . . . taken advantage of. That is something I do not tolerate."

"We only want what rightfully belongs to us!" Arica cried, her own voice ringing shrilly in her ears. "And Raden lied to you! He's not the rightful heir to

Connor made a sound like someone trying unsuccessfully to breathe under water.

the throne of North Bundelag. He was banished by the Fairy Queen, and he has no claim upon the throne or the book!"

Haggdorn stopped in front of Raden and frowned. "Is this true?" he demanded. Arica actually thought she heard his voice rise a notch or two.

"Yes, my mother did ask me to leave the country for a brief time," Raden admitted, smiling greasily. "But what is a little disagreement, now and then, between a mother and a son? It means nothing. A family matter, as you said yourself."

"Nevertheless, I dislike being lied to," Haggdorn replied. He turned back to Arica, his smooth, plump face as placid as ever. "I will give you the *Book of Fairies*. I'll provide food for your journey home, a few coins and even a horse to ride. You may take back whatever you brought with you, including the sword. However, there is a price — a rather large one, I'm afraid. I am a businessman, after all."

Needles of ice prickled over Arica's skin.

"You must leave Shadow with me. I desire very much to be the only man in South Bundelag to own a unicorn. He is my price. You can have some time to think it over, but don't take too long. I might change my mind."

"You can't own a unicorn," Arica managed to choke out. "They belong to no one." Out of the corner of her eye she glimpsed her uncle's eyes upon her, dark and mocking, but he said nothing.

"If it's true that you speak to unicorns, then why don't you ask Shadow what he wants?" suggested Haggdorn.

Chapter 9

The two moons hung like silver pendants against a black sky spattered with stars. Arica walked slowly through the grass as though every step brought pain. She could have called out to Shadow with her thoughts, and would probably have received an answer. But she wanted to see him with her own two eyes, stand face to face with him and tell him she had no right to trade away his freedom, not even for a hundred fairies' lives. For though he was not all good, his life — any creature's life — was not hers to give away. She and Connor would have to find another way to get the book.

As she neared the stable, she saw that Shadow

was not inside his stall as she had expected, but waiting for her inside the fence that surrounded the pasture. She paused and breathed in the scent of freshly cut hay, horse sweat and manure. She had always loved the smell of these animals, for there was nothing else like it, in her own land or any other.

Your thoughts spill unhappy secrets to the wind, he said. Was it her imagination, or a trick of the moonlight, that he no longer looked so thin? He reared, threw back his head and pawed at the air. His dark horn glittered like red sparks spinning around a flame.

Ride me, True One, he said.

She hesitated, and he drew closer. She took his head between her hands and stroked his face and nose, then rubbed the itchy place behind his ears. "I can't let Haggdorn have you," she said. "You are a creature of light and magic, meant for freedom and wide open spaces."

Shadow pulled back from her touch, his dark eyes bright with that old, deep rage. *The Fairy Queen offered me a place at her side in the Fairy Village if I would come here and help bring back the book,* he said. *But I could never be happy and accepted in North Bundelag. Since arriving here, I have realized that this is the only place where I can find peace. I am accustomed to the ways of humans. I cannot read Haggdorn's thoughts, nor he mine, but I understand human language, and he spoke to me tonight of his wishes. He will be a good master.*

"But a unicorn should never have a master!" she cried.

It is my choice, True One. Will you ride me one more time? It is my final gift to you.

She climbed upon his back with a heart made of lead, and no, it had not been her imagination. The bones pressed less sharply through his skin as he broke into a gallop. She leaned forward and grasped a fistful of mane while the ground sped by beneath them, faster and faster. The wind whipped her hair into a thin stream behind her and brought the tears rushing to her eyes.

She had not realized a unicorn could run with such speed. The air roared in her ears. The breath was snatched from her lungs even as she tried to draw it in. Yet still his pace increased.

Now for the magic, said Shadow, and the world went still.

Then he was no longer galloping over the rough, rocky ground that rattled her bones each time a hoof struck down, but on moonbeams soft as silk. They glittered beneath and around her like the flutter of silver birds above a silent sea. Joy rushed through her soul, the joy of freedom and of cares long forgotten. It was like someone had placed her and Shadow inside a huge, clear bubble, then turned down the

Joy rushed through her soul, the joy of freedom and of cares long forgotten.

flow of time. Ever after she would remember that for one glorious minute, she and Shadow soared above the world. A little farther and they might have reached the stars. It was a precious gift, indeed.

Then they were pounding across Haggdorn's pasture once again, and the stars gleamed far above them, and the moonbeams were only pale glimmers in a cold and distant sky. She dismounted and walked back to Haggdorn's house slowly, with an aching sadness inside of her for what might have been.

Arica and Connor left the next morning just as the sky began brightening into dawn. True to his promise, Haggdorn filled their bags with food for the journey, returned the sword and provided them with a horse — though not much of one. Connor took one look at the small, sway-backed roan mare named Stitch and turned away in disgust.

"We might as well piggyback on a snail," he muttered to himself. Arica remained silent, as she didn't figure they were in any position to be ungrateful.

Something told her things would not go smoothly on their journey home, however — and unfortunately, she was all too right. By the time they reached the streets of Mulek ten minutes later, Stitch had already thrown a shoe. It took them an hour to find a blacksmith. A few more hours went by while they waited for him to get the job done. After that they were hungry, so they stopped just outside the city by the edge of the road to eat. Then Connor discovered he had to go back for his bundle, which he swore he had left at the blacksmith's. It took quite a lot of insisting on Connor's part to convince the man that the bundle was there and not somewhere else entirely, but finally his oldest daughter produced it with apologies, and they were on their way again.

Stitch's cross-country pace turned out to be slower than her city one. They were only a few kilometres out of town when it was time to stop for supper.

"At this rate, we'll be a whole month on the road," complained Arica between bites.

"I have an uneasy feeling about all of this," said Connor. "Why didn't Raden put up a fight when Haggdorn gave away the *Book of Fairies*? It all seems too easy, somehow."

"I wouldn't exactly say it was easy," disagreed Arica. "Have you forgotten the inn and the dungeon?"

"I mean after that. Once we found the book, it seemed like Raden just . . . gave up. He didn't even get angry when you accepted Haggdorn's price — I'm sure he thought you wouldn't do it. It's almost like he wanted to get rid of us."

Arica reached into her pack and drew out the *Book of Fairies*. "Now that you mention it, one thing has been bothering me, as well," she admitted, flipping through the pages. "Grandmother believed that when I found the book, I would feel the fairy magic. Maybe it has been in South Bundelag for so long that all the magic drained away. I certainly don't feel anything special. It is a beautiful book though, don't you think?"

"I haven't looked at it yet," said Connor, and held out his hand.

Arica stretched out in the grass while Conner perused the book. She yawned enormously. It would be nice if that little round cloud up there would just move over a bit and cover the sun . . .

She woke to a pink sky in the west and her cousin with his nose still in the book.

"Why didn't you wake me up?" she cried, as she leaped to her feet and brushed away some scavenging ants. "It's almost night!" A few metres away, Stitch blinked and flicked an ear lazily in her direction.

"I've been reading the *Book of Fairies*," explained Connor, "and there's something about it that isn't quite right. In fact, I could almost go so far as to say something is very, very wrong."

"Connor, we've got to get going!" she wailed, grabbing things and stuffing them into her bag.

"How badly do you think Raden wanted the *Book of Fairies?*" Connor asked in a voice too quiet for her liking.

She froze, her hand still partway inside her pack. "Very badly. Why are you asking?"

"Badly enough to make a fake one?"

"Are you saying this isn't the real *Book of Fairies?*"

"What better way to get rid of us quickly than to make sure we found what we were looking for?"

Arica shook her head. "He could have just booted us out of the city without Shadow *or* the book."

"Would you have gone?" Connor asked.

"Not without a huge fight. And not for long, either. I'd come back until I got it. Or Grandmother would."

"My point exactly," said Connor.

"You could be right," Arica admitted. "But I can't believe Raden would go to all that trouble. The book looks so . . . genuine. Names and everything."

Connor shook his head. "But at least one name is missing. The Fairy Queen said that all living fairies are listed in the book. I've read every name in the list, and Theodore Warman — your grandfather's name — isn't here. Yet your grandfather specifically told us he was still alive."

"But no one knows except us and Grandmother," said Arica. "Everyone else thinks he's dead . . . " and then her voice trailed off. Her stomach felt sick.

"If you were Raden," went on Connor, "and you wanted to make a fake book really quickly, what would you do? I don't know about him, but *I'd* throw in a few real names — the obvious ones like yours and your father's and the Fairy Queen's — and then I'd start pulling names from any old place, like the phone book, for example."

"There are no phone books in Bundelag," said Arica miserably.

"You know what I mean," said Connor. "This book is fake, Arica. We have to go back to Haggdorn's house tonight, no matter how badly we want to stay away, and find the real *Book of Fairies*."

Chapter 10

The minute they turned back, Stitch began to move twice as fast. Still, by the time Arica and Connor arrived at Haggdorn's backyard night had fallen, leaving them with a day completely wasted and another needle to find in an even bigger haystack.

They tied Stitch to a tree beside the pond. It was the same place Drusa had hidden her pony the day before. Both moons were covered in drifting clouds, but the light of lanterns flickered from nearly every window of the house.

"It seems like all we ever do is sneak around this yard in the dark," muttered Connor as they stumbled toward the stable, not daring to use the flashlight for fear of being seen. "I'll be lucky not to trip and break my neck."

"Stay here by the door," instructed Arica as they neared the long red building. "I'll go inside and see if Shadow is in his stall. If someone comes, warn me by howling like a wolf."

"I don't know how to howl like a wolf," protested Connor. "Can't you come up with a better plan? People only do things like that in movies."

"You'd be surprised what you can do when the pressure is on," she said, and slipped inside the stable.

Shadow stood and watched her come, as if he'd known all along that she would. He tossed his head, his ears perked and pointing toward her. She stopped a metre back, not daring to touch him. If she touched him her anger would melt away, taking her resolve with it.

"Did you know the *Book of Fairies* was a fake?" she asked, her words dropping hard and fast as rocks.

Silence hung in the air between them. Somewhere by Shadow's hooves a small animal squeaked and scurried away. From deep within the stable came the sound of thudding hooves and the whinny of a restless mare. Outside, the wind whistled thinly through the trees.

Yes, I knew, Shadow said at last. *I overheard the human and the fairy making plans.*

"Why didn't you tell me?" she said, trying to keep the heartbreak out of her voice.

What are you so upset about? You knew all along you couldn't trust me.

She swallowed, feeling something raw and sticky in her throat. He was right, of course . . . for the first time, she saw how right he was. She saw that he knew how to stay silent when he should speak, and how to avoid answering when telling the truth did not suit him. He had learned to hide the truth. He could never return to his own kind.

"Do you know where the real *Book of Fairies* is hidden?" she asked.

I have chosen not to get involved in this. His thoughts rang coldly in her brain.

"You are already involved," she said, and walked away. The exchange had taken less than a minute, and with any luck, she would never have to see this unicorn again.

The next moment a sound like the shriek of an angry cat pierced the quiet night air. Arica tore down the length of the stable and burst out through the doorway. Connor sat on the ground with his bundle clutched to his chest. A young male elf stood over him, pointing a large, three-pronged pitchfork at his throat.

The elf — obviously one of Haggdorn's stable boys — turned his head when he heard her and there they remained, sizing one another up in uncomfortable silence. Arica recognized him as the elf they had seen here once before. After a long moment the pitchfork slid back to the ground and he addressed her.

"My apologies," he said. "I know who you are, now. You're those friends of Perye's." He paused, puzzlement creasing his brow. "But I thought you left this morning."

"We did," Arica told him, "but then we discovered that the book Haggdorn gave us is not the one we came for. Have you heard of the *Book of Fairies*? Do you know where it is hidden?"

The elf boy shook his golden head. Green eyes glowed at them through the darkness. "No, I don't," he said, "but good luck in your search, and don't get caught. My master doesn't like to be crossed. And be sure to stay away from dark barns," he added with a chuckle and a wave of his hand. Then he stepped inside the stable and was gone.

"That was a close one," said Connor as they made their way back through the trees and along the shore of the pond. Water lapped peacefully by their feet. Offshore a small fish glinted for one brief instant, then disappeared with a sound like the bursting of a bubble. Overhead, one of the moons peeked bravely through the scudding clouds, then hid its face once more.

"The Fairy Queen said you would feel the book's magic," rambled Connor, voicing his thoughts out loud. "Do you think she was wrong?"

"She was wrong about Shadow. Why not about this?" Arica replied, her voice hard even to her own ears. Immediately, she was ashamed.

Connor paid her no attention. "You should try to remember all of the times you encountered magic in this place," he said. "My guess is that Raden hid the book somewhere out of the way, thinking you could never get near enough to feel it. It's probably out here in the yard somewhere. At least, that's where I would hide it."

Magic in this place? She hadn't felt any, except that final time on Shadow's back, and that was now too painful to recall. But something else was nagging in the back of her mind. There was another time, wasn't there? Oh, yes. When she burned the dungeon door with her father's sword. But that was the sword's magic, and didn't count. And then once more . . .

"Connor!" she gasped, trying to get a yell and a whisper out all in one breath. "Follow me to the big oak tree!" Then she took off running.

They arrived in only minutes, and the first thing she did was rush up to it and fling her arms around its enormous trunk. The tingling went through her body in one great rush, nearly taking her breath away. Connor stepped up close beside her and pressed his own body to the wood.

"It must be pretty powerful magic," he said after a moment, "because even I can feel it. It's a bit like pins and needles all over my body, only much more pleasant."

"Let me stand on your shoulders," she said to him. "There must be a hole up there to hide things in."

Sure enough, after a few minutes of fumbling around amid the leaves and branches, her hand came into contact with a long narrow opening, just the right size for a book. She reached inside and was not surprised when her fingers closed over a cover of hard, smooth leather. Pulling it out of its hiding place, she gazed at it for a brief but joyous moment. She handed it down to Connor, then struggled to keep her balance as his shoulders started wiggling wildly beneath her.

"What are you doing?" she hissed.

"Getting the fake book out of your pack to put in the real one's place," he explained.

Connor's hand came up holding the fake book *Book of Fairies*. "And hurry, will you? You're not exactly a featherweight, you know. My shoulders feel like all the skin is scraped off. Couldn't you have worn softer shoes?"

"Well if you'd put on some weight, it would help a lot," she retorted, then added, "Sorry about the shoes."

. . . her fingers closed over a cover of hard, smooth leather.

Climbing down turned out to be the most difficult part of all, ending with the two of them flat on their backs in a tangle of arms and legs.

When they had themselves all straightened out, Arica peeked into her pack once more to make sure the book was really there.

"Now let's get out of here," said Connor.

Stitch was right where they had left her, still chewing and blinking sleepily in the darkness. That explained the great, sagging belly, anyway. They threw everything onto her back and clambered aboard. They gently nudged her sides but the mare refused to budge. They not-so-gently nudged her sides, with no better success. Connor dismounted, took the reins in his hands, and pulled. The animal planted her feet and pulled back. She was safely home at last, and no one was getting her to go anywhere tonight.

"Let's just leave her," said Connor. We can probably travel faster without her, anyway."

Arica shook her head. "Haggdorn will find her in the morning and know we came back. Since we'll be walking, he'll catch us in no time."

"That is a problem," admitted Connor.

They stood for a while in silence, mulling over the problem. Leaves whispered in a sighing breeze. Moonlight grew brighter around them. They lingered in a glow that steadily increased. Arica stiffened. Connor sucked in air, then let it out slowly, a little bit at a time.

"That light isn't coming from the moons," Arica said.

"Don't move," he hissed at her. "Maybe it will pass by us, whatever it is."

The light drew nearer, and nearer still. They shrank back until they were hidden behind Stitch's body, and waited, hardly daring to blink. Arica was certain they were doomed — for who else but Haggdorn or Raden would be out with a lantern this late at night, skulking through the trees?

The next moment the bushes parted with a whisper and out from behind them stepped Wish the unicorn, pale as a white-cloaked spectre. Her horn glittered like whirling jewels as she came.

Chapter 11

Arica's first heart-sinking thought was that now Wish would be caught by humans and dissected for all her magic parts.

"Tell her to turn down her horn," whispered Connor in dismay. "Someone is going to see it and come running."

"Your horn, Wish," she said.

It was bright to find you, True Arica, she said, and the light dimmed. Arica threw her arms around the unicorn's neck and groaned. "Why did you come?" she whispered into Wish's neck. "I'm thrilled to see you, but your life is in terrible danger here."

You were in a dark, cold place, True Arica,

explained Wish. *I sensed your pain, so I came. Even my mother Song couldn't keep me away. Your life is in danger, too.*

Arica stroked the unicorn's face and sighed. "You've got me there," she admitted.

Connor tugged on Arica's arm. "Can't you see? This is the answer to our problem!" he exclaimed. "We can ride Wish out of here."

She opened her mouth to explain that Wish was too young and had never carried one person before, let alone two, but the little unicorn's thoughts came into her mind, clear and certain. *Don't worry, True Arica. I'm stronger than you think.*

Arica flinched as they climbed up on Wish's back, but she soon discovered her fear was groundless. Wish moved through the yard and onto the road smoothly and without apparent effort. As she walked, her horn continued to fade. Then it disappeared altogether in a tingle of magic, just like Shadow's had done.

Nevertheless, Arica saw that Grandmother was right. Even on a dark night like this Wish could never pass for an ordinary horse. Every flawless, glowing part of her revealed the truth of what she was.

Even when they had left the city, Arica couldn't relax. They rode quickly and in constant fear, stopping to rest no more than two hours at a time. They didn't dare start a fire in case it drew unwanted attention, so everything they ate was raw or cold or both, and they had no way of warming themselves when the sun went down. Connor didn't seem to mind. He declared he loved camping, and the flies and filth didn't bother him in the least. But Arica hated every dirty, dreary minute.

By late afternoon the second day, Arica could no longer ignore what she had been aware of for some time: that someone was following them. At first, the dust off in the distance had seemed far enough away to be of little concern. Arica was sure they would lose their pursuers once they left the road, and so for a while she didn't even bother to look back. But as they neared the border, she sensed the bitter touch of Shadow's mind upon her own. Wish flicked back her ears and said, *Shadow the unicorn is behind us, True Arica.*

Evening came, and with it, the next problem. The singing of the river hit her like a deluge, filling her with the maniac desire to run plunging into its cool depths.

Try to keep still, True Arica, said Wish sympathetically.

Arica tried, but the restlessness seemed to jump off her and onto Connor like a flea. He kept leaning forward, pushing against her back.

Arica turned to scowl at him. "Connor, could you

please — " She stopped, aghast. Their pursuers were now close enough to be seen clearly. One of the animals was dark in colour, and the other a pale grey. The grey one hadn't bothered to hide his horn, just as Wish was no longer covering hers.

Wish broke into a gallop, and Arica had to clamp her teeth together to keep from shouting at her to go faster.

Connor had no such care. "Hurry, hurry!" he cried, seeing — as they all did — that they were never going to make it.

Then she looked ahead, across the river into North Bundelag, and saw the Fairy Queen galloping full tilt toward them on one of her huge, grey stallions. Even from this distance she could see Grandmother's mouth open in a silent shout of warning. But Grandmother would never make it here in time to stop Raden from overpowering them and taking back the *Book of Fairies*, or from doing whatever else he had in mind.

Wish strained beneath them as the ground flew by faster and faster, but to no avail. The riders on her tail drew nearer and nearer. Now Arica could make out the individual features of the two men. Arica wondered how her uncle had managed to get Haggdorn off his precious unicorn and onto the tall bay stallion instead. Perhaps it had been Shadow's idea, to make his betrayal complete.

The roll of their pursuers' hoofbeats on the road grew louder as they neared the place where the invisible bridge was — at least, thought Arica grimly, she hoped Wish had got it right. On the other side of the river, the Fairy Queen was bearing down over her stallion's neck, her long purple robe billowing behind her.

Now Arica could hear the slap of Haggdorn's leather saddle and the panting of his exhausted mount. Both of the unicorns breathed lightly still, though the froth gathered on their mouths as much as it did upon the horse's.

"Give me the book, you little thief!" shouted

Raden behind her. If she had any breath, she might have laughed out loud at who was calling whom a thief. She wondered why he hadn't brought his gun. She could be thankful, at least, that there were no bullets zinging past her head.

"I'll jump off!" yelled Connor in her ear. "Wish can run faster with only one rider!"

"No!" she shouted back. "Raden would grab you!"

Haggdorn's stallion fell back, unable to keep up the pace. Only Shadow ran beside them now, nose to nose with Wish. Raden's dark eyes blazed; his lips twisted in rage as his hand groped like a claw for her pack and the book that lay within it.

. . . his hand groped like a claw for her pack and the book that lay within it.

Arica looked over at Shadow as he strained beside her and remembered another, much happier ride. The animal lifted his head, and as his gaze met hers she spoke — whether in her head or aloud, she would never know.

"I thought you weren't going to get involved," she said.

He gave no answer, but as his gaze broke away from hers, she thought she saw a glimmer of regret deep in his eyes. Then the tip of Raden's fingers brushed against her pack — and Shadow the unicorn stumbled and fell, taking Raden down with him.

Arica heard Raden's final scream of fury at the same instant that the bridge blinked into sight and Wish's hooves thudded upon the first boards. Up, up they went, over the slope of the old wooden bridge and down the other side into North Bundelag. Still Wish did not pause, but tore wildly on until she reached the place where the Fairy Queen raced to meet them.

Arica looked back just as Shadow and Raden scrambled to their feet. The look on her uncle's face was not something she would like to see again any time soon. It would stay with her long, she was certain, and visit her often in her nightmares.

Then Raden dashed toward the bridge, and she knew she could not let him cross it.

As she had done once before, she drew the magic from Wish's horn until she held within her cupped hand a ball of glittering blue that throbbed like the spitting ends of live wires. Then she reached back, and sent the ball hurtling through the air with all her strength.

The bridge groaned and creaked, as if inflicted with some unendurable pain, then exploded upward in a funnel of splinters and dust that rained down into the frothing stream below. And when it was over, there was only the great, orange sun sinking slowly in the west, and the River of Songs calling out her name.

Epilogue

The following day Arica stood beside the doorway to Earth with Wish, her cousin Connor and her grandmother, the Fairy Queen of North Bundelag.

"I have one question for you, Grandmother," she said. "Why did you send Shadow with us?"

The queen's sigh was whisper-sad, like feathers brushing over silk. "I knew he couldn't be trusted," she explained, "but I hoped that the good in him would win out over his anger and his bitterness."

"You took a great risk."

The Fairy Queen nodded. "But I knew his anger was no longer directed at you. Think back. Did anything good come of it?"

Then Arica remembered a ride of wild joy through a starlit sky filled with moonbeams and magic. She recalled his sudden fall at a time when it seemed that all was lost.

"Yes," she had to admit.

Grandmother turned to Connor. "Thank you for your help in bringing back the *Book of Fairies*," she said. "The creatures of this land owe you a great debt. But you must go. Arica will stay behind a moment longer, for she has something more to do."

Connor nodded respectfully to the Fairy Queen, then turned to go. He took a few steps, stopped, breathed in deeply and turned around. He pushed his glasses back up his nose and gazed at her in an eager, pleading way.

"I would like to come back to Bundelag soon," he said. "I've been happy here. It's different from at home. The kids there make fun of me. I don't have any friends really, except for Arica. But here, everyone accepts me for what I am. They actually like me — the unicorns, the elves, the trees and rivers, everyone."

Arica figured now was not the time to tell him about the trolls.

Grandmother smiled. "The only sure thing about tomorrow is that nothing is certain," she said wisely. "I can't promise anything, but the things we set our hearts on and work for often have a way of coming to pass."

"I felt needed here," he told her. "I helped do something good."

"And maybe you will again," the queen said, and bent and kissed him on the cheek. "Goodbye, dear boy."

Arica stepped forward and gave her cousin a hug. "Thanks for everything," she said. "I couldn't have brought the *Book of Fairies* back without you. I'll see you soon. You're the best, and don't let anyone tell you any different."

He grinned back at her. "You bet I won't," he said, with more happiness in his voice than she'd ever heard.

Then Wish, not wanting to be left out, snorted and bounded forward.

"Goodbye, Wish," Connor said, throwing his arms around the unicorn's neck. "I'll miss you a lot." Reluctantly, he broke away. Then he raised his arm in farewell and stepped toward the door.

After Connor had gone, Arica reached into her pack and brought out the *Book of Fairies*. As always, the magic of it tingled over her skin and through her veins like fire. Grandmother took the book and held it to her breast for one long moment, then spoke.

"You and Wish must do this together," she said. "I am hoping that the magic of the book combined with the magic of the unicorns — that magic of purity and truth — will awaken the lost fairies to the truth of who and what they are. Are you ready to try?"

Arica nodded eagerly, and Grandmother placed the book back in her hands.

The real book was not black but brown, and the writing within was not done in Raden's spidery scrawl but in a clean, clear script. At the front of the book were recipes, and although Arica had never heard of a single ingredient, she knew exactly what they were and where to find them. Next were the fairy laws, full of fairness and truth. Then came the spells, which she knew would flow like music from her lips if she spoke them.

Last of all were listed the names of all the living fairies. She skimmed them, the Fairy Queen looking over her shoulder. There was Theodore Warman, right where he should be; and her father's name, and Raden's, and her own. She looked up at Grandmother, eyes shining.

"So the magic is still there after all these years," said Grandmother, her voice full of emotion. "And . . . look down the page a little farther."

Arica almost dropped the book into a patch of shrubbery, for there, plain as the nose on a frog's face, was printed the name of her totally human cousin Connor, the one who had followed her through the crack between the worlds.

Next were the fairy laws, full of fairness and truth.

"No, it can't be," she said, her tongue moving thickly around the words.

"And why not?" asked Grandmother. "There were signs of it, weren't there? I noticed something unusual about him the moment he stepped out from behind the tree. After the initial shock of seeing me, he adjusted like he had been here all his life."

She thought about the *Book of Fairies* in the oak tree, and how her cousin had felt the magic there. She remembered how the River of Songs pulled at him just as it pulled at her. "Connor can't possibly be a fairy," she said stubbornly. "His mother and my mother are sisters, and they are completely human!"

"That may be so," pursued the Fairy Queen, "but what about Connor's father?"

Arica stared back at her, aghast. "Uncle Fred?" she cried. "But he's the most unmagical person I know! He clumps when he walks and snores in his sleep! He laughs like a donkey! Why he — he makes noises when he eats!" she concluded, not knowing how better to explain the impossibility of it all.

Grandmother scowled, looking like a black cloud had settled just above her head. "Do I detect a bit of snobbery here? What makes you think you can look at the outside of a person and tell what he is really like? If you have learned anything these past few months, I hope it would be to always look into a person's heart."

"I'm sorry, Grandmother," she said meekly.

Unexpectedly, Grandmother laughed, and the black cloud cleared. "Enough lecturing! I have been waiting for this moment for so long, Arica. Open the book to the page where the names begin. The magic of the fairies will tell you what to do next."

So Arica sat in the forest beside the doorway to Earth while sunlight sparkled off the leaves and danced across the ancient, yellow pages in her hands. Wish stepped close beside her and reached down to touch the pages with her horn, bathing them in blue. As Arica read each name out loud, the magic thrilled along her veins and seeped into her bones. When she was done, she knew exactly what to say.

"Fairies everywhere — come home."

Vicki Blum lives in High River, Alberta, with her kids and her pet snake. She works with books as an elementary-school librarian, and enjoys doing workshops with young writers. The first two books in her series about Arica's adventures in Bundelag are *Wish Upon a Unicorn* and *The Shadow Unicorn*.

When Arica falls through a crack in her grandmother's kitchen floor, she finds herself in a strange world of fairies, trolls, elves and — best of all, unicorns.

But the trolls and their evil master, Raden, take her prisoner, just as they have the unicorns. Fortunately, Arica discovers that she can hear the thoughts of the unicorns, in a way that no one else in this world seems able to do.

With the help of Wish, a playful young unicorn, Arica sets out to free the captives — and discover the true reason she was brought to this magical land.

Wish Upon a Unicorn
by Vicki Blum
ISBN 0-590-51519-5
$4.99

Through a half-open window the wind moans, as if in pain. *Help us, True One,* it seems to say, as it whispers through the leaves.

So begins Arica's return journey to the magical land of unicorns, fairies and trolls. She arrives to find that the evil Raden is on the loose once again. With the help of a traitorous unicorn named Shadow, he has turned all the other unicorns to stone — all except Arica's friend, Wish.

Now it's up to Arica and Wish to stop them, and to bring the unicorns back to life.

The Shadow Unicorn
by Vicki Blum
ISBN 0-439-98706-7
$4.99